Who Stole
Uncle Sam?

The Chickadee Court Mysteries

WHO STOLE UNCLE SAM?

MARTHA FREEMAN

CHICKADEE COURT MYSTERY #3

SCHOLASTIC INC.
New York Toronto London Auckland Sydney
Mexico City New Delhi Hong Kong Buenos Aires

Acknowledgments

I am beyond grateful to Dr. Sven Bilén of the College of
Engineering at Penn State, to copy editor extraordinaire and
Yankee fan Nancy Smith, and to Bill Bown, manager of the
2007 State College American All-Stars, for helping me
with the specifics of this manuscript. Any errors are,
of course, my own.

M. F.

ISBN-13: 978-0-545-12338-9
ISBN-10: 0-545-12338-0

12 11 10 9 8 7 6 5 4 3 2 1   9 10 11 12 13/0

Printed in the U.S.A.   40

First Scholastic printing, November 2008

For the State College American All-Stars, 2007

Dieter Bahr

Dalton Bown

Scout Droske

Ethan Frank

Dan Fry

Darian Herncane

Jon Herzing

Saige Jenco

Greg Kellar

Jake Matty

Nick Rose

Connor Shadle

Nick Smith

Chapter One

It was the top of the sixth, and the score was 5–0.

I don't need to tell you we were losing. We were always losing.

There were two outs, and nobody was on base. The count was 0–1 on the big blond kid. If he hit a grounder, the play would be to me at first base. I was praying for a strikeout. Even a walk. Anything so I didn't have to run after a bad throw for the sixth time that afternoon.

Our pitcher, Joey, went into his windup; he threw. . . . The blond kid swung and connected, a bloop pop-up that dropped into no-man's-land between the pitcher's mound and second base.

"First!" I yelled.

Andrew, the shortstop, got the best jump on the

ball, ran over and knelt to retrieve it, but Joey was there at the same time. They collided, and Joey fell backward onto his rear end. In the process, he kicked the ball, which rolled innocently toward Conor, the second baseman. But Andrew didn't see it. He was frantic, spinning around, waving his arms. Finally Conor dived for the ball, but in the process he tripped over Andrew's outstretched glove and did a somersault.

It was better than circus clowns.

The home-plate umpire even laughed.

By the time Andrew finally got his glove on the ball, the blond kid had been relaxing at first for about half an hour, but Andrew was pumped and threw to me anyway—threw right over my head. What a surprise.

By the time I trotted back from the parking lot with the ball in my glove, Coach Banner had called everybody to the mound.

"What game are you guys playing?" he asked in the super quiet voice that meant he was trying hard not to holler. "Dodgeball maybe? Now get back out there and play baseball the way we've coached you!"

It was a Sunday afternoon in May, and the sun was warm and bright. I could feel a layer of sweat between my skin and my shiny jersey. Trotting back to the field, I glanced over at my parents in the stands. They were easy to pick out because my dad was next to my mom, and my mom was behind a fat newspaper. My mom loves me and all, but she says her life is busy and she has to multitask if she's going to get everything done.

My team is Uncle Sam's Lawn Care. That's a stupid name for a baseball team but only a little stupider than Itzinger's Auto Parts, the team we were playing that afternoon. In PYB, Pennsylvania Youth Baseball, the teams carry the names of the businesses that sponsor them.

Besides my parents, my other fan is Yasmeen, who comes to games with her gloomy genius little brother, Jeremiah. Yasmeen is my next-door neighbor and my best friend who happens to be a girl. The reason she comes to my games is that Jeremiah is weird for a six-year-old, and she thinks exposing him to some normal thing like baseball will make him less weird.

Yasmeen is also the person who helps me solve mysteries—I mean, the person who *used* to help me solve mysteries. We are not going to do that anymore. We made a pact.

In PYB teams play only six innings. Our team

was home that day, and we went down one-two-three in the bottom of the sixth. There was a little excitement at the very end when Andrew hit a fly almost to the fence, but the guy in center caught it for the third out.

End of game.

Of course we didn't score any runs. Sometimes I'm amazed we make any outs when we're in the field. I am an average ballplayer. I can throw and I can catch and so long as I don't have to run very far, I'm not that slow. But on my terrible team that's enough to make me a star. The only kid better than me is Josh, the coach's son. He can pitch a sixty mph fastball, he can catch, he can hit the ball a mile, he can run the hundred in twelve seconds.

You might be wondering, if we have a player that good on our team, how come our record was zero wins and eleven losses. It's because Josh only gets to play the minimum. See, he and his dad don't get along, and to punish him his dad makes him sit out.

We high-fived with the other team—"good game," "good game," "good game"—then jogged out to left field to talk it over like always. While we jogged Coach Banner came along behind us, like a cow dog nipping at the herd's heels.

"Move it! Move it! Move it! Get those rear ends in gear, boys!" he hollered.

Josh wouldn't jog with the rest of us. He walked. In a way I couldn't blame him. Like usual he played the least that PYB rules allow. Even Troy, the worst player on the team, usually plays more.

In left field we dropped to the grass. "Hey—did you see on *SportsCenter* last night about how they might pay us to play baseball?" Mitch asked me.

"Pay *this* team?" I said.

"Yeah, I saw that," Conor said. "These guys in Las Vegas want to set up some kind of pro league for kids. Recruit the best players and pay them, charge admission to the games—all that."

"*Sweet!*" Andrew said. "If we were on TV, Conor's somersault over me today would've been all over the web!"

"All right, listen up," Coach Banner hollered. "That was a disappointing loss; but the foe was formidable, and I see some signs of improvement. I think we can still get ourselves some wins this season."

"Right," Josh mumbled.

"Did you say something, Josh Banner?"

Josh looked up at his father. "Coach, we are

never gonna win a game. We're all losers. You too. Now can everybody just go eat?"

Coach Banner's face got pink, and he took a couple of steps toward Josh. The rest of us looked at our shoes and the bugs in the grass.

"Settle down, Sam," Coach Hathaway, the assistant, reached forward and touched Coach Banner's shoulder.

Coach Banner whirled around. "Keep your hands to yourself!"

Coach Hathaway kept his voice even. "The boys are hungry," he said. "And their parents"— he nodded in the direction of the bleachers— "would like to get home."

Coach Banner gave Coach Hathaway a laser-death stare. But before he could say anything, Conor, our round-bellied second baseman, let loose with one of his trademark belches. We couldn't help but laugh, even the coaches.

"Excuse me," Conor said, which made every-body laugh again.

Coach Banner took a breath like laughing had been what he needed. "We'll get 'em next time, guys," he said. "Okay—go on and get something to eat."

I ran to the concession stand, thinking Josh was

right behind me, but when I turned to say something, he was gone, walking toward the parking lot where his mom was waiting in an Uncle Sam's Lawn Care truck. It was red, white, and blue with a winch on the back like a tow truck, and a tank and hoses with sprayers for Uncle Sam's famous Red-White-and-Blue lawn-care formula. Mrs. Banner was in the driver's seat, reading a book.

Naturally if I was going to play baseball this year, I had to get assigned to what my dad calls a "dysfunctional" team. *Dysfunctional* means "something that makes everybody who's a part of it crazy." Usually people talk about dysfunctional families, is what my dad explained to me. He knows this kind of junk because he has read every book there is on how to raise kids and be a good parent. This is why I, his only child, am so wonderful.

Anyway, that's what Dad says.

On our team it's not only Josh and his dad who don't get along; it's the coaches, too—Coach Banner and Coach Hathaway.

Coach Banner is a Marine Corps veteran. He's so patriotic he dresses up like Uncle Sam for holidays. Coach Banner is also super-organized, even his gym bag. He keeps spare baseballs, clean socks, power bars, and a first-aid kit—all in their own compartments. Coach Hathaway is the exact opposite. He used to be a hippie, and he's proud of it—still has long hair and a little gold ring in his left ear. He can never find his mitt or his car keys.

Coach Banner owns a big business, and he makes tons of money and lives in a big house. He drives a red sports car if he's not driving one of the company trucks.

Coach Hathaway teaches at the college, a subject called sociology, which means he tries to understand how groups of people behave. He has bumper stickers about Native Americans and petroleum all over his old truck, which is rusting on the bottom, and there are so many books piled in it you can barely fit a passenger.

The only thing they agree about is baseball. They both love baseball.

Yasmeen came up behind me in line at the concession stand.

"Good game," she said.

"Right," I said.

"No, really," she said. "You didn't get ten-runned. That's like a victory for you guys."

Ten-runned is when the other team's ahead by

ten after four innings, and they call the game so it doesn't get so sad that the losers all start to cry.

"You had a walk and a single, and you made two outs," Jeremiah said. He showed me his score-card, like I might not have believed him without proof. "That makes your career batting average .327, and your on-base percentage .460. I wish you guys would get some runs; then I could calculate RBIs, too."

I got my burger and an orange Gatorade and headed over to a picnic table to sit with Conor and Andrew and Mitch. I was halfway there when Teresa and Ashley intercepted me.

"We saw your *picture*." Ashley giggled. She and Teresa are two girls in my grade who wear charm bracelets and nail polish and sparkly shoelaces on their clean pink sneakers, and usually come to the baseball games. I can't figure out why. They don't watch. Instead they get candy at the concession stand, walk around and around the field and through the parking lot, giggling till the game's over. Then they come over and bug us players.

Yasmeen can't stand them.

Right then I didn't know what they were talking about. "Huh?"

"Your picture with *Yasmeen*," Teresa said. "Is she your *girlfriend*?"

There was a positive eruption of giggles.

It came to me what she might be talking about. A couple of months ago, this lady from a magazine interviewed Yasmeen and me about the two mysteries we've solved together. Then a photographer came to my house and took pictures of us with my cat, Luau.

"Yasmeen looks so *pretty*," Ashley said. "Luau looks sleek and orange and handsome, and you look . . ." She and Teresa looked at each other. More giggles.

What is it with some girls anyway?

Chapter Two

At our house there's a mail slot in the front door, and when the letter carrier pushes the mail through, it lands on the rug in the hall. Lots of times it sits there for hours before anybody picks it up. But that day when we got home from the baseball field, Luau was sitting on the rug where the mail was. And when he saw me, he started circling and swishing his tail and mrrrfing.

This was unusual cat behavior even for my unusual cat.

I bent down to scratch behind his ears. "What is it?"

Luau bumped his head against my palm: *Take a look at* this!

Lying there on the floor was the new issue of

College Springs Magazine, and—*oh my gosh*—Yasmeen and Luau and I were on the cover!

I grabbed the magazine off the floor, which caused Luau to complain, *Hey, I wasn't done looking at my handsome self yet!*

I was afraid to take a good look, so I squinched my eyes shut and peeked through my lashes. Luau was draped on the arm of our sofa with a sleepy expression on his face, Yasmeen was sitting on the sofa with a half-smile on her face. And me?

It was worse than I could have imagined: I was staring straight at the camera like a scared kindergartner in his first school picture—a big painful smile pasted under my nose.

I thought fast. Whatever happened, I had to get rid of this picture before anybody else saw it. My dad was in the kitchen, and my mom had gone upstairs, so I rolled up the magazine, hid it under my uniform jersey, and headed toward the back door. The trash barrels are just outside.

Luau meowed in protest. *I want that framed and hanging over the fireplace!*

I had only taken a couple of steps when my dad came in, blocking my way. "Oh, the mail's here," he said, and went around me, picked it up, and shuffled through the envelopes. Luau meowed again, *Look at what Alex has hidden under his shirt!*

Dad looked down at him, then up at me. "What's the matter with your cat?" he asked.

"Probably hungry," I lied.

Dad looked at me quizzically. "Do you have something under your shirt, Alex?"

My mom had been coming down the stairs as my dad spoke. Now she said, "What's up?"

"Nothing." I took a couple more steps toward the door. "I'm just, uh . . . going out to the, uh . . . car. I forgot something."

"He's got a salmon hidden under his jersey," Dad said.

Mom held out her hand and smiled. "Did the magazine come?"

"How did you know?" I asked and— miserably—brought it out from under my shirt and handed it over.

"Beth Ryan called this morning to tell me the magazine was coming out today and that you were the cover story," she explained. "She knows Jana, the editor, from church." She looked down at the cover, then up at me and grinned. "Awww, Alex. What a handsome kid you are."

She showed it to my dad, and he smiled, too. "You got your mom's looks—thank goodness."

How could anybody—even parents—see that picture and think I looked good? Then I had a horrible thought: Maybe in real life I look worse!

Luau meowed again. This time it was obvious what he was getting at.

"And you're a very handsome kitty, too," Mom said.

My dad studied Luau as he stretched out on the floor. "On the other hand," he said, "that belly of yours is looking rather ample these days, Luau. Time for the low-cal cat food?"

Mom bent down to give him a tickle. "The vet says he's on the heavy side of the chart."

Luau purred. *Oh, please. I've got washboard abs. They're just obscured by all the fur.*

"He could use some exercise, too," Dad said.

"Kitty treadmill?" Mom asked.

Dad laughed. "Actually I thought I might try walking him."

"What?" I said. "Dad, you can't walk a cat! Everybody will laugh. Can't we just let him out more often?"

"That's not such a good idea, honey," Mom said. "You remember what happened at Halloween—when he disappeared? That was pretty scary. He's safer if he's an indoor cat."

"And what do I care if people laugh?" Dad asked.

Luau swished his tail, which meant, *You may not care, but I have my reputation to consider.*

I thought about my own reputation, which was shot now that everyone in town was going to see this photo of me. "So you knew about this magazine cover all day?" I asked Mom. "Why didn't you *warn* me?"

"At least somebody notices when you do good work, Alex," Mom said. "In fact, I can't help feeling just the tiniest bit jealous."

"Jealous?" I said.

Mom shrugged. "You and Yasmeen have solved two tough cases. That's great, and I am one hundred percent proud of you. Still, I solve a couple of cases every month. And nobody's putting me on the cover of a magazine."

"I know you're a good detective, Mom," I said. "And you'd look a lot better than me in this picture."

Dad put his arm around Mom and kissed her ear. "You're the best detective in College Springs," he said.

15

Mom laughed. "Also the only one with a badge." She mussed up my hair the way I hate, then looked at Dad. "I've got to run downtown."

"The federal thing?" Dad said.

Mom gave Dad a raised-eyebrow, pursed-lip look that could only mean, *You're not supposed to talk about that in front of Alex.*

So of course I asked, "What federal thing?"

"Oops," Dad said.

"Yeah, *oops.*" Mom frowned at Dad, then turned to me. "Never mind, sweetie. I'll be back soon. Then I'll have a cup of tea and read about my son, the star detective."

Chapter Three

The next couple of days at school were weird. Everybody treated Yasmeen and me like we were famous or something. Thank goodness it didn't last. By Wednesday Yasmeen and I could eat lunch together without Teresa or Ashley making jokes that we're a "celebrity couple."

On Friday, Yasmeen and I walked home from school together. On the way we walk by Bub's, which is on the corner of our street, Chickadee Court. Bub is an old guy who lives by himself. His house isn't as nice as the others, and some of the neighbors get annoyed because he doesn't always mow his grass in summer or shovel the snow in winter. But Bub keeps soup on the stove for anybody who drops by, and he's our friend. Once he saved Yasmeen's life. And he has helped us solve a couple of mysteries, too.

That day there was no baseball practice, but we had a game the following Monday, Memorial Day. Uncle Sam's Lawn Care would face Belletoona Pets & Fish at Saucersburg at one o'clock. The annual Saucersburg 5-K Race was that same morning, and I was planning to watch, so it was going to be a busy day. Yasmeen had been training for the race and might even get a ribbon.

"Come in. The bell's busted again," Bub called when we knocked on his front door. We walked into the tiny hallway and turned right into Bub's messy living room. The house smelled like soup. Bub was sitting, like usual, at his dining table, which is at one end of the living room, near the door to the kitchen. The TV was on with the sound on mute.

"You should get Sofie to come over and fix the doorbell," I said. Sofie Sikora is a year younger than me and some kind of electronics genius. She lives on our block, too.

"I've been waiting for her to drop by," Bub said. "Till she does I reckon people can knock. It's split pea today, by the way."

"I'll try it," I said, but only because I was really

hungry. I am not so crazy about split pea soup. It's the color that gets me. But Bub is a great soup-maker, and I hadn't eaten since two bologna sand-wiches, some chips, an apple, carrots with ranch dressing, and cookies at lunch.

"So how's the life of the famous kid detec-tives?" Bub asks. "Solved any murders lately?"

"Not you, too," I said.

"Alex hates being a celebrity, but I don't mind as much," Yasmeen said.

"Don't mind? You like it!" I said.

Yasmeen shrugged and looked embarrassed—but only a little. "I guess I kind of like it," she admitted. "Some of my relatives from Trinidad called. They read the story on the web."

Yasmeen's dad is from Trinidad. He has this cool accent that makes him sound smart even if he's only talking about whose turn it is to clean the tub.

"My sister read it and e-mailed me, too," Bub said.

The magazine had called Bub our "unlikely inspiration and mentor." It mentioned some of the other people on our street, too, including Sofie Sikora because she helped us solve the Halloween mystery.

"Have some more soup," Bub said. "Hey—and, young lady, aren't you runnin' that race on Monday? You need somethin' that'll stick to your ribs."

This time I served the soup. When I came back to the table, Yasmeen was telling Bub about her training for the run.

"Tell me again how fast you have to be to win the age group," I said.

"Eight-minute miles," Yasmeen said. She has always been a fast runner. But her running as a sport is new. She started after her dad decided to try it last winter, and now they're both serious.

Bub laughed. "It takes me eight minutes to get up and get to the bathroom." Bub patted his belly, which is about the same size as his soup pot.

"You should come to the race," Yasmeen said. "My dad's running, too, and Alex will be there."

"You're not running, are you, Alex?" Bub asked.

Of course I wasn't running. Around the bases is plenty far for me. But I was a little insulted that Bub asked the question like he *knew* I wouldn't be running. "I've gotta play baseball afterward," I said. "I wouldn't want to be all tired out."

"In that case the two of us can spectate together," Bub said.

Yasmeen grinned. "That would be *great*."

"What's the matter with this doorbell anyway?" a voice called from the front porch.

"Come on in, Fred,' Bub called back. "It's busted again."

Officer Fred Krichels walked into Bub's house. He stops by for soup pretty much every day. He is a patrol officer with the College Springs Police Department. Even Bub admits he's not the sharpest blade on the Swiss Army knife.

"Hey, kids," he said. "Nice article about you two. I never realized you had such a handsome mouthful o' teeth, Alex."

"The soup's split pea," Bub said.

"My favorite!" Officer Krichels said, which he says about all of Bub's soups. He kept talking as he headed into the kitchen. "I was a little disappointed, kids, that the article didn't mention yours truly." There was a pause as he dished up his soup; then he came back into the living room and set his bowl down. "I fully realize it was the so-called *novelty* factor, two youngsters such as yourselves who have assisted us police a time or two. Still, you have to admit, without my dogged detective work, neither of the perpetrators in question would have been brought to justice."

I knew Yasmeen was itching to tell him that he *never* would have solved those cases without us. But Officer Krichels is Bub's friend, plus he works with my mom. So before she could open her mouth, I changed the subject.

"Are you really going to come out to the race, Bub? Maybe Professor Popp could drive you, too," I said. "You have to be ready at seven-thirty."

"I'd love to hitch a ride with you folks," Bub said.

"The Saucersburg 5-K on Monday?" Officer Krichels said. "I'm thinking of doing that myself."

Bub was surprised. "Running, Fred? You?"

Officer Krichels wiped his mouth with his paper towel. "I been meaning for a while to take up running. Everybody says I got the physique for it."

Officer Krichels's physique looks like it was put together with pipe cleaners. Bub clamped his mouth shut and laughed with his eyes. Yasmeen busted up.

Officer Krichels frowned at Yasmeen. "We'll see who's laughing on Monday at the race, my girl."

Yasmeen folded her arms across her chest. "How many training miles are *you* running?"

"I don't need training miles," Officer Krichels said. "Police work is physically demanding. I am in peak condition."

"So you think you're going to beat me on Monday?" Yasmeen said.

Officer Krichels leaned back in his chair and nodded.

"You want to place a wager on that?" Yasmeen asked.

"I'll take that wager," Officer Krichels said.

"A box of Pirate Crunchies," Yasmeen said, "my favorite training cereal."

"Hey, I *love* those things! Especially the ones with vanilla minichips." Officer Krichels put out his hand, and the two of them shook. The bet was on.

Chapter Four

My alarm went off at six forty-five on Monday, which was a holiday, which just goes to show you what an excellent friend I am. On the bed next to me, Luau stretched and swished his tail. *Time for breakfast?*

When Luau and I walked into the kitchen, the coffeemaker was burbling on the counter, and Mom was watching, like watching would make it burble faster.

"Good morning, my handsome son. Good morning, Luau." She poured herself a mug of coffee and sat down at the table. "Tell Yasmeen and her dad to run a little extra for me."

"Will do," I said. Then I went to the cupboard for Luau's kitty chow and saw that Dad had bought a different kind. It was in a green bag that said "specially formulated to slim down your feline fatty" on the front. I poured Luau a bowl of the new stuff and explained, "It wasn't my idea."

Luau looked up at me, then down at the food. It wasn't as pink as the usual stuff, more grayish. He sniffed it, then took a step backward like it smelled bad. *Surely you jest, Alex.*

Mom had been watching. "Paws down on the low-calorie food, huh?" she said.

Luau sat down next to his food bowl. He doesn't do the laser-death stare as good as my mom does it, but he tried, which made my mom laugh. She took a sip of coffee, and I asked her, "Is that your *whole* breakfast?"

"It's my provisional breakfast," she said.

"You're worse than Yasmeen," I said. "What's *provisional*?"

"It means it's my breakfast until I think of a better breakfast," she said. "What time do you have to be at the Popps' house?"

I looked at the clock on the stove. "In about fifteen minutes," I said. "Are you coming to the game later?"

"Wouldn't miss it," she said. "I've got a week's worth of newspapers to catch up on."

"*Mom!*" I said through a mouthful of cereal. "You know, you and Mrs. Banner are the only parents who ever read at the games."

"At least I get out of my vehicle," Mom said. "Marguerite acts like she's too good for the rest of us parents."

"She's just not that into it because Josh never plays," I said.

"Maybe," Mom said. "Or maybe she's avoiding your dad."

I took two more big bites, and my cereal was gone. "Why would she do that?"

"You never get over your first love, Alex." Mom tapped the side of her head. "That's a little maternal wisdom to file for later."

"First *love*?" I frowned. "Yuck, Mom. What are you talking about?"

"Don't you remember about your dad and Marguerite Banner way back when?" Mom said. "How he broke her heart? There're photos in the album, not to mention our college yearbooks."

Mostly what I remembered about those old pictures was that Dad had really funky hair. But now that Mom mentioned it, there was some girl in some of them, too. Then later there was a different girl—Mom.

"Do you mean Maggie? Dad's old girlfriend?"

"She's a lot thinner now, and of course all the makeup and jewelry and toenail polish," Mom said. "So you might not have recognized her. Maggie *is* Marguerite Banner—Mrs. Banner. Back in the day she and Dad were sweethearts."

"You're kidding!" I said, then I thought of something. "Hey—does that make Josh and me cousins?"

Mom laughed. "I don't think so, and anyway it's ancient history. He broke up with her their senior year, and then he started dating me."

I got up to put my bowl in the sink. A second later Dad walked into the kitchen. He must've heard the last part of the conversation because he said, "One of my better decisions."

It's always a little freaky to think that your parents had lives before they had you. Like, if Dad had married somebody else, there wouldn't be a me, right? Or would there be a me, just not a me in this house with these parents?

These thoughts were too big for my average-size brain, so I asked my dad why he had broken Mrs. Banner's heart.

"Yeah, why?" Mom asked, teasing. "Was something wrong with her?"

Dad sat down and pulled the newspaper toward him. "I dunno," he said. "I guess because she was too smart for me."

"I think I'm insulted," Mom said.

"No, no," Dad said quickly. "*You're* too smart for me, too, Noreen."

Mom said, "Well, all right then."

Dad grinned. "But Maggie was so ambitious," he went on. "I mean, she got a PhD at twenty-five, became a professor. . . ." He shrugged. "Then she invented that Red-White-and-Blue formula that kills bugs—and she got rich."

"And it all could have been yours," Mom said.

Dad shook his head. "I'm not the businessman Sam is. It's the two of them together that built the little empire they've got going. Like I said, sweetheart, I made the right decision." He smiled at Mom, and she smiled back. It was gross, to tell you the truth. I looked at the clock again. I had about thirty seconds to get to the Popps' house.

"Gotta go—*bye*!" I sprang out of my chair.

Closing the front door I heard my dad say to my mom, "Say—how does Luau like that new food?"

Chapter Five

A few minutes later Professor Popp pulled his big gold SUV into Bub's driveway. Yasmeen hopped out so Bub could get in front, but Bub waved her back and heaved himself into the backseat next to me instead. "Happy Memorial Day!" I said.

Bub chuckled as he pulled the seat belt around his big belly. "I'm not sure 'happy' is the right way to put it for Memorial Day."

"You mean because we're still stuck in school for two more weeks?" I asked.

Professor Popp smiled at me in the rearview mirror. "This is a somber holiday, intended to remember soldiers who died fighting for the ideals of this country," he said. "It is a day for patriotism and reflection."

Professor Popp is an English professor. He knows a lot. And Yasmeen's mom is a librarian, so what he doesn't know, she can find out.

"Bub was a soldier," Yasmeen said.

"Ah-yup," said Bub. "An airman."

We passed the grocery store and the McDonald's that are by the College Springs city limits. Next we'd go by a cornfield and a cow pasture, and then the dairy where we buy our milk. After that we'd go under the highway; then we'd be in Saucersburg.

"I had understood you were a veteran," Professor Popp said to Bub. "Vietnam, correct?"

"Ah-yup," Bub said. "Air Force. I flew the B-52 out of Guam."

"You were a pilot!?" I asked.

"A gunner," Bub said.

"That's amazing!" I said.

"What's amazing?" Bub said. "Did you think I was always a fat old man?"

"*Hey*," I protested. "I didn't mean it that way."

"Yes, you did," Bub said. But he punched my shoulder, which was his way of forgiving me, while at the same time reminding me he's about five times my size.

We pulled into the parking lot at Saucersburg

30

Park, which is where the baseball fields are, too. It's a really big park with a grove of trees, picnic tables, and two little-kid playgrounds on opposite sides.

Even though we were half an hour early, about a zillion people in running clothes were already there. Some were sitting on the wet grass stretching, some were in line under a sign that said REGISTRATION at the picnic pavilion, and some were lined up for the Porta Potties by the parking lot. The craziest ones were jogging. Can you believe it? They were here for a race, and instead of resting up like sensible people, they were tiring themselves out by doing unnecessary extra jogging!

We got out of the car and walked over onto the grass. "They need more o' those bathrooms," Bub noted as we walked by.

"There are some over there." I pointed across the park to another row way beyond the baseball diamond. Nobody was in line over there. Too far away.

Professor Popp went over to the picnic pavilion to sign in. Yasmeen and Bub and I found a sunny spot on the grass so Yasmeen could do warm-up stretches.

"Hey, Alex!"

I looked around and saw Coach Banner. He waved and walked toward us. Uncle Sam's Lawn Care not only sponsors my team, it also sponsors the Memorial Day race. Every year Coach puts on his Uncle Sam suit and rides a decked-out bicycle ahead of the runners.

Coach Banner wasn't in his Uncle Sam suit yet. He was wearing black sweatpants and a white short-sleeved T-shirt. His arm muscles were straining against the sleeves.

"Beautiful day for a race," he said. Then he dropped down on the grass next to Yasmeen, Bub, and me. "Still got to lace up my shoes." He pulled a pair of red-white-and-blue bike shoes out of his gym bag, then he retrieved a plastic bag full of shoelaces. Most of them were your basic black or white, but one pair was sparkling silver.

"I only use these silver ones for Memorial Day," he said. "I get years of wear out of 'em that way. You running in the race, Alex?"

I shook my head. "Saving my strength for baseball," I said. "I came to yell for my friend, Yasmeen. She's gonna win a ribbon!"

Yasmeen looked embarrassed. "Well, *maybe*, Alex," she said. "Hi, Coach Banner."

"Well, of course I know Yasmeen. I read all

about the two of you in that magazine, and I've seen you at baseball games, haven't I? You two must be pretty loyal friends."

I introduced Bub, and he and Coach Banner did their nice-to-meet-yous.

"Marine Corps?" Bub said to Coach Banner.

"How did you know that?" I asked Bub.

"Well, for one thing there's the insignia on that gym bag o' his," Bub said. "And for another . . ." He grinned and touched his own hair, what there was of it.

Coach Banner rubbed his crew cut. "Once a jarhead, always a jarhead," he said.

"You serve in the Gulf?" Bub asked.

Coach Banner nodded.

"Air Force," Bub said. " 'Nam. We were having ourselves a little history lesson in the car coming over here. Seems these kids don't know what Memorial Day's all about."

"Up to us to tell them then, isn't it?" Coach Banner said.

"Ah-yup," Bub said.

Coach Banner had finished lacing up his shoes, and he stood up. "Gotta go do the Superman thing," he said. "Transform myself from mild-mannered businessman into Uncle Sam!"

Yasmeen and I laughed. "But there's no phone booth," she said.

"True," Coach Banner said. "So I'll have to use Superman's traditional backup—the Porta Potty."

I made a face. "Yuck."

Coach Banner flexed his biceps. "I'm a man; I can take it," he said.

"But look at the time!" Yasmeen said. "You'll never be ready."

"I've been doing this for years, remember, and I always use the ones over there—across the park," Coach Banner pointed. "No waiting, and I get a little warm-up jog before I hop on the bike."

Coach Banner left. Meanwhile Professor Popp came back from signing in with two little chips that looked like guitar picks. Once the chips were threaded in a runner's shoelaces, the sensors in them would keep track of the runner's times.

Yasmeen fixed the timing chip in her shoe; then stood up. "We better get over to the starting line," she said. "I am *so* excited!"

Lined up for the start of the annual Saucersburg 5-K, Yasmeen and all the other runners bounced around like hot popcorn kernels. Looking at them for one insane moment, I wished I was running, too.

Bub must have had the same thought because he said, "Looks kind of fun, doesn't it? If I was twenty years younger . . ."

"There's guys your age running," I pointed out.

"Let me amend that statement," Bub said. "If I was twenty years younger and fifty pounds lighter . . ."

"Look—there's Officer Krichels, right at the front!" I pointed. Officer Krichels was right up against the starting tape with a bunch of thin guys with strong-looking legs, most a lot younger than he. They all had fancy running clothes, too, shiny sleeveless mesh shirts, dinky shorts, spotless shoes.

Officer Krichels was as skinny as the rest of them, but his legs looked like matchsticks with kneecaps. And instead of shiny running clothes, he was wearing a ratty T-shirt that said GREEN ACRES IS THE PLACE TO BE and old black gym shorts.

I wanted Yasmeen to win her bet, but I almost felt sorry for him. He looked like somebody's beat-up old junker in a race with Corvettes.

But then Officer Krichels waved at me and hollered, "Hey, Alex, where's your girlfriend?"

And I didn't feel sorry for him anymore.

Bub answered. "Yasmeen and her dad are

starting a ways back in the pack, Fred. But watch out. They look *fast*."

Officer Krichels hollered, but I couldn't understand him because at the same time there was an announcement on the loudspeaker. It was something about Uncle Sam reporting somewhere. His bike, I noticed, was still leaning against a tree.

Bub looked at his watch. "It's a few minutes before eight," he said. "That's strange. Your coach is usually a stickler for punc—"

I am pretty sure the rest of that word was going to be "tuality," but there's no way to know for sure. It never got out of Bub's mouth. Instead something happened right then that set off a string of events so amazing that even now I have a hard time believing it ever happened.

What cut off the end of Bub's word and delayed the Saucersburg 5-K was a colossal *boom*—a *boom* that echoed all over the park and over to Mt. Lyon and back again. A *boom* that was followed by about a zillion little *pops*, each one representing a puff of brilliant and colorful sparks.

"The fireworks shed!" somebody shouted. And without thinking, Bub and I joined the crowd running across the park toward the noise.

Chapter Six

The fireworks for the Fourth of July display in Saucersburg are stored in a big metal shed at the park. Something had touched off an explosion there, and now the fireworks were doing a full-out, unauthorized, preseason display all on their own. I have to say, it was freaky to see fireworks flowering, cascading, and erupting in daylight—with blue sky and sunshine in the background.

The fastest runners got to the shed quickly, but the sparks, fire, heat, and smoke pushed them back. Then over the *wheee!* and the *whizzzzzz!* and the *pop!* of roman candles, I heard the growl of a siren revving up. Next thing a Saucersburg fire engine was rolling over the lawn past me. No surprise that the volunteers got here fast. The fire station is only about half a block away.

In the next half hour, more fire engines came and ambulances and police cars, too—including my mom. She had heard about the explosion on the police scanner and she was worried about me and Yasmeen.

"*Mom!*" I protested. She was almost strangling me with her hug. "I'm *fine*! Everybody's fine, I think."

My mom didn't let go. "I see you're fine, honey," she said. "But I'm holding on anyway."

By this time the fireworks had stopped popping. Yasmeen, Mom, and I walked over toward the shed. All that was left of it was a messy, smelly, wet pile of black wood and metal with steam rising off it. Firefighters and police wearing shiny protective gear, helmets, and boots were walking over the wreckage. No one else was allowed to get close.

"So much for the race, I guess," Mom said.

"No, Mrs. Parakeet, they're still going to have it!" Yasmeen said. "At least they're going to try to. I heard the guy with the starter pistol talking to another guy. He says the park's big enough they can keep this area taped off, and the race goes off in the other direction."

"That's great," Mom said. "I know how hard you and your dad have trained, Yasmeen. Maybe I'll stick around, and—"

"Detective Parakeet?" A police officer I didn't know waved at Mom.

She closed her eyes for an instant. I knew that expression. It meant, I really wasn't planning on working on my day off. But then she opened her eyes, straightened out her frown, turned, and said, "Hey, Joe—what can I do for you?"

"Have you got a minute to take a look here?" the officer asked. "Since you're on the scene anyway . . ?"

Mom told him sure. Then she went off to help with the investigation, and Yasmeen and I looked around for Bub.

"The race is on!" Yasmeen told him.

"So I hear," Bub said. "But there seems to be one problem: No one can find Uncle Sam."

"Wasn't he on his way to change into his outfit?" I asked.

Yasmeen nodded. Her eyes were glittering. This was not good. "What do you say, bud?" she asked me. "Wanna go see if *we* can find him?"

"That wouldn't be detecting, would it?" I asked. "Because we have an agreement about detecting."

"Of course it's not detecting," Yasmeen said. "Follow me!"

She took off running, and with no choice, I jogged after her. It turned out she was going to the far side of the park by the alley where there was that row of Porta Potties, the place Uncle Sam had been heading earlier to change.

"Look at this," she said. On a low branch, Uncle Sam's hat and beard were hanging.

"He must've left them there before he went in to change his clothes," I said. "But why didn't he ever take them back?"

Yasmeen removed the hat and beard from the branch. She looked worried. "Alex, what if there's something wrong?" she asked. "What if he's still in the Porta Potty?"

We looked at the row of blue boxes. There were four of them in a line on the gravel by the alley. Something seemed funny about them, different from before. But what would be different about Porta Potties?

"Go over there and knock," Yasmeen said.

"Why am I the one who has to knock?" I asked.

"He might be sick, Alex!" Yasmeen said. "Would you please *hurry*!"

I folded my arms across my chest. "If you're so worried, then why aren't you the one knocking?"

"Because Coach Banner is a *boy*!" Yasmeen said. "And it is not appropriate for a *girl* to be going after a *boy* in a Porta Potty!"

I tried to find a way out of this logic, but I couldn't, so I walked over and climbed the two steps to the first door. Then I noticed something— the little red sign above the knob said "occupied." Maybe Coach Banner really was in there! "Hello?" I called. "Coach?"

"Try louder!" Yasmeen said. "Try the door!"

I didn't want to, but now I was worried, too. I pushed on the door, and to my surprise it opened right up—and nobody was there.

"Try the next one!" Yasmeen said. "Hurry!"

So I did, and it was the same story, and for the others too. The sign said "occupied," but the door opened, and no one was inside.

Weird.

We didn't know what else to do, so we ran back across the field and found Bub.

"No luck, I see," he said.

"How do you know?" I asked.

Bub tapped the side of his head. "Power

o' deduction," he said. "Yasmeen's holding the Uncle Sam beard and the Uncle Sam hat. Ergo: lack of Uncle Sam. Maybe you'd better report your findings to the professional." Bub nodded at Officer Krichels who was coming toward us from the direction of the fire.

"Ask me what?" Officer Krichels said.

We showed him the hat and beard and explained. But instead of giving us advice, Officer Krichels laughed. "Now that you're famous, you kids want to see mysteries everywhere, don't ya. I'd say it's unlikely anybody *stole* Uncle Sam, wouldn't you? I'm sure Sam Banner will be back in plenty of time to lead the runners on his bicycle—just like he does every year."

I really wanted to believe that Officer Krichels was right, but the sad fact is that Officer Krichels is almost never right.

Chapter Seven

The annual Saucersburg 5-K Run, delayed by the mysterious explosion at the fireworks shed, was now set to begin at eleven. By ten forty-five even Officer Krichels was wondering where Uncle Sam had gone. He called Marguerite Banner, Sam's wife and Josh's mom—not to mention my dad's ex-girlfriend—on her cell phone. She and Sam had come to the park for the race early that morning, but she said she had lost track of him in all the excitement after the explosion. She had gone home to check on Josh, who had slept in, but now she was on her way back to the park.

"ETA five minutes," Officer Krichels told Bub and me when he hung up. "You know, Saucersburg is too dinky to have a PD of its own, so they have an agreement with our department to do the protection and investigation. Your mom's gone back to the station, Alex, so I'll be the one to get this particular investigation rolling."

Yasmeen and I looked at each other. We were both thinking the same thing: Uh-oh.

When Mrs. Banner drove up, she was in the coach's red convertible—not the Lawn Care truck like usual. I couldn't help wishing my family had a car like that. Riding in it would make even a dork like me look good.

The race organizers huddled with Mrs. Banner for a few minutes under the picnic pavilion, and then there was another announcement on the loudspeaker. The race was a go for sure, but with the usual Uncle Sam missing. Did anybody want to volunteer for the job?

"It's a fine patriotic tradition," the announcer said, "and it would be a shame to let it lapse. Volunteers, please report to the man with the starter pistol."

Bub had been relaxing on the grass in the sunshine; but as the announcement was made, I saw he was listening intently. And when it was done, he began the cumbersome process of getting his big body vertical.

"Where are you going?" I asked him.

"Gimme that hat," he said. "Please."

He nodded at the Uncle Sam hat in my hand.

"Why?" I asked.

"Because how often does a patriotic fella like me get an opportunity to impersonate Uncle Sam himself?" Bub said. "And on Memorial Day, no less."

I couldn't believe it. "Bub, you *can't!*"

Bub placed his big paw on my shoulder. "Weren't you the one telling me, Alex, that I should get with an exercise program? I can't do anything about being old, but it's time I started working on being *fat*. Besides, it's my patriotic duty. Yoo-hoo?" he hollered. "Mr. Starter? You've got yourself a brand spanking new Uncle Sam!"

I wasn't any too sure about this. But when I handed Bub the Uncle Sam hat, and he set it on his head, it fit fine. In fact it even kind of went with his outfit. Bub always wears jeans, a plaid shirt, and red suspenders. The starter looked doubtful; but Bub turned out to be the only volunteer, and everyone was eager for the race to get going.

At about two minutes to eleven, the runners were lined up, bouncy as before with Officer Krichels at the starting line, and Yasmeen and her dad a ways back in the pack. Bub was getting ready to jump on Uncle Sam's bike about fifty yards down the lane ahead of the runners.

"Ready, Bub?" The starter yelled at him.

Bub touched the brim of the Uncle Sam hat perched on his head, stepped down on the pedal of the specially decorated red-white-and-blue bike, and rode away down the course.

"Runners, take your marks. Get set, and—"

Pow! The starting pistol went off. I opened my eyes and saw a flash of color as the jackrabbits zipped past. Behind them came a slower mass of confusion, the runners jostling each other, trying to break out of the pack. In there somewhere were Yasmeen and her dad.

I couldn't see them, but I yelled anyway: *"Go, Yasmeen! Go, Professor Popp!"*

Bringing up the rear were runners and walkers with dogs, with strollers, with little kids skipping beside them. A little boy was crying; he was the only sensible one in the whole bunch if you ask me.

A fast runner can cover a three-mile course in less than eighteen minutes, and of course the idea was that Bub on the bicycle would stay ahead of the runners. I looked at my watch and figured Bub would be back easy by eleven twenty. There was time for me to go get a drink of water. I turned toward the fountains, but then I heard my name being called.

I look down the block where the last of the slowpokes were rounding the first corner and disappearing from sight.

"Alex! Over here!"

What the . . . ? It was *Yasmeen's* voice, but at first I couldn't see her. Then I jogged a few yards up the lane where the runners had gone and saw her in the shadows on the sidewalk. Bub was with her! Both he and the bike were leaning against a tree.

"What happened?" I ran toward them. "Are you all right?"

Bub looked dazed. The Uncle Sam hat was still on his head but tilted to one side, and one suspender had slid off his shoulder. "Those kids are *fast*," he said.

"They caught up to you, huh?" I said.

"Mowed down is more like!"

"But what are *you* doing here?" I asked Yasmeen. "What about the race? All that training, and—"

"It doesn't matter," Yasmeen said.

"She stopped to help me. I told her to move along, but she insisted," Bub said.

"You can go *now*," I told her. "You'll pass plenty of people if you do."

Yasmeen shook her head. "No point," she said. "It's okay."

That's what she said. But you could see in her face what she *felt*, and it was big-time disappointment. She acted all businesslike, though—took Bub's elbow and said, "Come on. Let's get you back to the park."

"You kids go," Bub said. "I'm gonna finish what I started." He grabbed the handlebars.

"Get out!" I said. "You're going back to the park with us and find a nice bench and sit on it. I'll get you some water."

Yasmeen and I argued, but Bub wouldn't listen. He waved us away, pushed the bike into the street, swung his body over the seat, and pushed off down the racecourse. "I'll be fine now that the runners are past," he called. "See you at the finish line!"

Yasmeen looked at me. "We can't let him go by himself."

"I was afraid you'd say that," I said.

"You don't have to come," Yasmeen said.

I sighed. "If something happens he'll need both of us."

Yasmeen grinned. "Try to keep up, okay?" And she ran off to catch Bub on the bike.

Yasmeen is such a fast runner and Bub is such a

slow bike rider that the two of them were side by side when I rounded the corner and saw them up ahead. Already my chest hurt, my legs hurt, and my eyes were tearing. Bub's face was pink, and he was sweating; but he seemed to be rolling along fine.

"Are you sure . . . you're okay?" I asked him between breaths.

"It's easier . . ." Bub was panting, too, "than mining coal." That had been Bub's job when he was a young guy and there were still lots of coal mines in Pennsylvania.

Bub and I were both too winded to talk, but beside us Yasmeen chattered like we were relaxing around Bub's table. She told us about Jeremiah's new teacher and about her plans for our big end-of-the-school-year assignment, which is called the Decades Project. Every once in a while, either Bub or I grunted to show we were still alive. Soon we passed a mom pushing twins in a stroller, and then we passed the dad with the boy who had been crying earlier. The boy was smiling now, but the dad didn't look so hot.

"Are we almost done?" I asked.

"We haven't even gone a *mile* yet!" Yasmeen said.

I didn't ask questions after that.

The Saucersburg 5-K course has one big hill

on it. I think it's called Mt. Everest. But there was a good thing about it. The up had an equal and opposite down. When we got to the water station at the bottom, I felt better.

And the last half mile of the race wasn't so bad. We were passing more people, which was kind of fun. Also spectators on the side of the road cheered for Bub, and all of us waved back. Finally we turned a corner, and I could see the finish line.

"You're doin' great! You're doin' great!" Yasmeen coached Bub and me.

There were a few runners ahead of us in the homestretch, and one of them had familiar matchstick legs.

"*Fred!*" Bub called.

Officer Krichels looked back over his shoulder. His face was pale. His hair was pasted to his head with sweat. His T-shirt clung to his ribs.

"Oh . . . hi," he gasped. "How much . . . farther?"

"Just up ahead," Yasmeen said, all perky. "You can do it, Officer Krichels! Follow me!" And she took off like there were jets on her shoes.

Officer Krichels put on two steps worth of speed, then dropped back.

Bub and I waved as we went by him. A minute later when Bub crossed the finish line, the crowd in the park went crazy. I pretended some of their cheering was for me, and we both waved at our fans. Then Bub rolled to a stop on the grass and sort of slumped off the bicycle. Someone handed us each a bottle of water and pointed us to tables where there were bagels and bananas.

No one had told me there would be food! Things were definitely looking up.

Yasmeen came over, and the three of us found a bench and ate bananas. We were almost done when Officer Krichels hobbled toward us.

"So how did you like running?" Yasmeen asked.

"It was awful," he said.

Bub laughed one of his great big belly laughs, a sound that told me he was truly feeling okay. Officer Krichels looked at Yasmeen sadly.

"I guess I owe you a box of Pirate Crunchies, little lady," he said.

"I wasn't really racing," she said, "so it wouldn't be fair for me to take your cereal."

Even Officer Krichels must've known that didn't make sense; but before he could answer, Mrs. Banner stepped up to the microphone at the picnic pavilion and said it was time for the awards ceremony. Usually Uncle Sam would give out the ribbons; but with him gone, it was up to her.

Now that I knew she used to be my dad's girl-friend, I looked at her a little harder than I had before. She was normal height with a normal body—not fat and not thin—and had curly brown hair. She wore eye makeup and bright red lipstick and big earrings and two gold bracelets and tight blue jeans. She sure was a lot different from my mom.

Still I felt bad for her having to talk in front of all these people when her husband was missing. She read a lot of names, and people came up to get their ribbons. When she got to "Males, 50-Plus," the first name she announced was: Derek Popp—Yasmeen's dad! We all whooped and applauded. Professor Popp tried to look modest when he collected his ribbon, but his smile gave away how proud he felt.

After all the awards were done, Mrs. Banner said that the baseball game would go on as scheduled, whether Coach Banner was back or not because, "That's the way he would want it."

There was more applause, and Yasmeen nudged me. "This is getting pretty mysterious, isn't it?" she whispered.

"I am not knocking on the doors of any more Porta Potties," I said.

Mrs. Banner wiped her cheek with the back of

her hand. Was she sweating? Or crying? You couldn't blame her. I wondered how Josh was feeling. Would he be up for playing ball?

Mrs. Banner looked down at the clipboard she was holding and said, "One last thing. The organizers of the fifteenth annual Saucersburg Memorial Day Run would like to thank everyone who stepped up to make this event a success in spite of the . . . uh, unexpected and difficult circumstances. In particular, we'd like to thank our substitute Uncle Sam, Bub Wisniewski. Bub?" She looked around. "Are you still here?"

Yasmeen piped up. "He's right here!"

Bub pointed at himself as if to say, *Moi?*; then smiling but a little unsteady on his tired legs, he made his way over to the pavilion. Mrs. Banner was holding up a Memorial Day Run T-shirt, size XXXL. The picture on the front was a cartoon Uncle Sam on a bicycle. She handed it to Bub and said, "On behalf of my husband and everyone here today, thank you."

There was more applause, and Yasmeen and I and Officer Krichels cheered: *"Woo-hoo-hoo!"*

When Bub came back his grin was ear to ear. "Lookit this." He held up his prize. "I got me a T-shirt."

Chapter Eight

With the excitement at the park and all the delays, I wasn't going to have a lot of time at home. Put on my uniform, grab my bag, eat a granola bar for strength, and head back for baseball.

"Thanks for the ride!" I told Professor Popp.

"Alex?" Professor Popp looked over the seat at me, then nodded toward my house. "What is it your father's doing there?"

I turned my head. My father was standing by the front steps. He didn't seem to be doing anything at all, but then I realized he was holding a leash, and whatever was at the other end of the leash had disappeared into the bushes.

Oh no.

"Uh . . . I'm not sure," I said, but as I spoke

Luau emerged from the bushes and tugged at the leash in my dad's hand.

Professor Popp is a little like Jeremiah. He doesn't laugh much. But when he does it's a very big laugh. That's the sound I heard now, accompanied by Yasmeen's higher-pitched giggling.

"Oh dear, Alex," Professor Popp wiped his eyes, "I am *sorry*, but I have never seen a man walking a *cat*!"

"Yeah, well," I said, "I guess we'll all have to get used to it"; and I jumped out of the car and charged up the walk.

"*Dad!*" I complained.

"What?"

"How can you do this to me?"

Dad smiled. "Right on target," he said.

I was in a hurry and already had the front door open. But now I stopped in my tracks. My dad was losing it. "Dad—what are you talking about?"

"I'm talking about *you*," he said. "You're right on target for healthy emotional development. A kid your age is *supposed* to be embarrassed by his parents."

"Is that from one of your parenting books?"

"Or maybe a magazine," Dad said. "*Whoa, Luau!*"

Luau tugged hard on the leash, yanking my dad

off balance. Dad did a pirouette trying to stay on his feet; but then the leash went slack, and Luau emerged with a wiggling lizard in his mouth.

"Yecch, Luau! Let him go!" I yelled.

Luau cocked his head and looked me in the eye. *If you aren't going to nourish me properly, I have no choice but to rely on my killer instincts.*

I didn't want to see what happened next, so I ran into the house and changed for baseball. When I came back downstairs, Dad was pulling the car out of the garage.

I threw my stuff in the back and jumped in. I was wondering about the poor lizard; but I didn't have to ask because Dad said, "I wonder how many calories there are in lizards."

On the way to Saucersburg—again—I filled my dad in on the race, and he told me he'd miss some of the game because it was his turn to grill burgers at the concession stand. Mom was still working, but she'd get to the game as soon as she could.

When Dad let me out at the park, I looked around for Coach Banner, hoping he'd be there safe and sound. But I didn't see him. Then Coach Hathaway announced he'd be in charge today. I couldn't help wondering if this meant Josh would get to play all six innings for once. But maybe Josh was too upset even to play at all. I didn't see him anywhere, either.

For a while the guys and I tossed the ball around to get loose. Then I saw Josh jogging onto the field. He was wearing his uniform. I looked at Conor, and I totally knew we were thinking the same thing: With Josh playing maybe we'd win for once!

I caught Conor's throw and trotted over. "Hey—how you doin', Josh?"

Conor was right behind me. "Is Coach back yet? Are you okay?" A couple of the other guys ran up, too.

"Nah, he's not back." Josh shrugged. "And like, I'm worried, but I can't do anything. So my mom said it'd be okay if I came down here and played. A distraction—you know?"

"So let's play then!" Joey said.

When our warm-ups were done, Coach Hathaway had a conference with Josh and with Kyle, who was supposed to pitch, over by the pitcher's mound. When Coach Hathaway came back to talk to the rest of us, he announced he was going to put Josh in as starting pitcher and save Kyle for relief.

"There's one thing, though, Josh," Coach

Hathaway added. "No back talk—not to me or the umpires or anybody. The minute you do, I'm going to pull you."

"I understand, Coach," Josh said.

All our games start with the national anthem played over the scratchy PA system. Since it was Memorial Day and everything, I actually thought about the words. I knew they were written when the British fired all night at this fort, and everyone was worried they'd shoot down the American flag. But in "the dawn's early light," the flag was still flying. Usually "The Star-Spangled Banner" is only the song before baseball; but on a patriotic day, it seemed more special. Or was it because Uncle Sam himself was missing?

We were the home team that day, which meant we batted in the bottom of the inning. After the players were introduced, Josh jogged to the pitcher's mound, and right away there was a buzz. The other team's coaches and scouts hadn't seen much of Josh; but they knew he was big, and they were worried.

Josh threw a couple of warm-up pitches that almost knocked our catcher, Presley, back onto his rear end. Then Josh nodded. He was ready.

"Play ball!"

The first pitch was a fastball, strike one. We all cheered, and so did our fans. Another pitch, another fastball. Strike two. Presley threw the ball back to Josh. I imagined myself as the batter facing Josh. If it were me, I'd swing this time, anything to avoid getting called out on strikes. Josh wound up, threw, and sure enough, the batter swung—but not like he meant it. The hit was a slow grounder back to Josh, who picked it up and lobbed it to me, an easy play. One away.

Josh struck out the next batter, and the third one hit a fly to John in left. Three up, three down. Our fans cheered like we had just won the state tournament.

Baseball should always be like this!

My team ran back to the dugout at top speed. We were psyched.

Unfortunately psyched didn't equal runs. Four innings went by with the score still 0–0. In the first I hit a long fly to right; but I swung late, and the right fielder caught it at the fence. My second time up, with one catch, I grounded up the middle for a single; then Joey moved me to second on a fly. But that was as far as I got because Josh hit a pop-up to short for the third out to end the inning.

"Sorry, man," he said as we headed to the field again.

"That's okay. We'll get 'em next inning."

But the truth was I felt bummed. If we couldn't win with Josh pitching a shutout, we really were losers.

Top of the fifth we were throwing the ball around the horn to warm up when I glanced over at the stands to see if Mom had come yet. Yes! She was there! So maybe the police had found Coach Banner? But if they had he'd be here, right? Or somebody would've come out to tell Josh, at least.

Also in the stands was a guy by himself I'd seen at a couple of games before. He stood out because of his clothes. They were always really colorful, Easter-egg colors. Today he had on a purple jacket and a light yellow shirt. He was sitting in the row above my mom, writing something. While I watched he leaned over and spoke to her, and she answered. What were they talking about? Who was he, anyway?

The first batter stepped in. Up till now Josh had been almost perfect, but his arm was getting tired, plus Pets & Fish was figuring out he likes to throw low and on the inside corner. This was their number-four batter, probably their best. I had a bad feeling. Sure enough he slammed the ball over Conor's head into center field. Mitch wasn't playing back far enough, and he had to run after the ball. The Belletoona coach swung his arms like a helicopter rotor, telling his runner to round first and keep going. By the time Mitch threw the ball to second, it was too late. A stand-up double.

"Shake it off!" Conor yelled at Josh.

"It's all you, buddy!" I chimed in.

"You'll get the next one!" I heard from somebody in the stands.

But Josh was rattled. The ball slipped a little on his next pitch and sailed high and slow toward the plate. The batter hit a solid grounder past the shortstop into left field. John fielded the ball and threw it to the cutoff man so the runner couldn't score. Runners at first and third.

Coach Hathaway jogged out to the mound to talk to Josh. I don't know what he said, but it worked. Josh struck out the next three batters, and that was the side. No damage. Bottom of the fifth, and we were up.

Unfortunately it was also the bottom of our batting order, and Troy was coming in for Andrew, who was batting eighth. Sam was the number-nine hitter. I'm first in the batting order, so I'd be coming up whatever happened. If I wasn't the third out (please don't let me be the third out), Joey and Josh would be up. Could I hope for a miracle? Didn't we deserve a miracle?

And what do you know, it looked like we might get one. Troy, smiling the whole time, hit a weird little dinker that bounced around the outfield like a jumping bean. The right fielder had trouble fielding it, so Troy, running flat out, beat the throw to second. Then Sam hit a grounder to the second baseman who threw Sam out at first, allowing Troy to go to third. One runner out and a runner on third.

I swung a couple of times in the on-deck circle, just to show 'em what they were up against. Then I looked at Coach Hathaway to see what sign he'd give me. He always throws in some nonsense to fool the other team, but there's what you call an indicator sign that means the next one is for real. Coach tugged his ear, tapped his nose, and clapped his hands. The indicator is a belly rub, but he never did that, so I was allowed to swing away. I stood in, adjusted my stance, and gave the pitcher my steeliest look. The ball came at me fast but low. Ball one. I took two more, not liking the looks of them, either; both balls. I checked the signs from the coach again. I didn't want to walk, but at this point maybe he wanted me to take the next one? Nope. I was free to swing.

The pitcher wound up, I took a look, and . . . I swung with everything I had. *Ping*—it was solid; I could feel it. I dropped the bat and ran, forgetting all about how my legs were half dead after the race that morning. The ball was sailing toward center. . . . Was it long enough? *Please* let it be long enough . . . *please.*

But no.

The center fielder had to go clear back to the fence; but he was there, and he caught it. I was out, but Troy tagged up and started for home. Oh *no.* Why did Coach Hathaway tell him to go, anyway? Troy's not fast enough to get to the plate against the arm on that center fielder; and if he was out, that was three! The cutoff guy was the second baseman. He snagged the ball, pivoted, and threw. It was gonna be close! The catcher was there, ready to tag; and Troy was pumping hard down the third-base line.

The throw was low. The catcher had to reach forward, and this slowed him down. I could hardly stand to watch, but the umpire was right there to call it—*safe!*

I breathed; then I hollered. The parents in the stands were going crazy. Even my mom—even Ashley and Teresa! I could hear shrieks. We were ahead! All the guys slapped me on the back.

"Great hit, Alex," Coach Hathaway said. "Okay, boys, we're not done yet. Joey, you're on deck. Let's see if we can get some more runs!"

Joey placed a grounder down the right-field line, Coach Hathaway waved him around first, and he slid into second for a double. When Josh came up he stood in the batter's box, stared at the pitcher, adjusted his stance, waited for the windup, and . . . slammed the first pitch over the left fielder's head, over the fence, over the bleachers where the parents were sitting. Oh my gosh—it seemed like that ball went over the moon before it crashed to earth someplace near the barbecue grill behind the concession stand.

No kid had ever hit a home run that far in Saucersburg. The guys on Pets & Fish looked stunned at first. But then one of their coaches started applauding, and pretty soon everybody on both teams was cheering—even the pitcher, who as of that day would go down in Youth Baseball history as the guy Josh Banner hit the amazing home run off of.

Josh didn't even showboat; he just ran around the bases smiling. We lined up and did the high fives the batter always gets after a home run—not something we'd gotten to do yet this season.

"Awright! Awright! Awright! Awright, *Josh*!"

Chapter Nine

Josh went on to get his shutout, so the final score was 3–0, Lawn Care over Pets & Fish. When we gathered out in left field after the game, Coach Hathaway congratulated all of us on the win, then said, "Let's dedicate it to Coach Banner, shall we, boys? He'll be back in action next week. I can feel it! Now anybody hungry?"

In a blink we were all up and running toward the concession stand.

But instead of getting in line, I ran around back by the grill where my dad was cooking. I wanted to ask him about Josh's home run.

"It came at me like a meteor," Dad said solemnly. "I think it was even glowing a little—from the heat buildup when it reentered the atmosphere."

"Right, Dad," I said. "Where's the ball now?"

Dad looked up from the burger he was flipping. "Mr. Shadle took it—you know, the president of the Youth Baseball commissioners. I think maybe they'll . . ." Dad's voice trailed off. He was looking over toward the parking lot. I followed his gaze. A bunch of little kids were standing in a semi-circle, staring at the Porta Potties on the other side, while two more little kids were running toward us.

"Something's going on," Dad said. He flipped the last burger onto a plate, closed the lid of the grill, waved at the kids, and started walking toward them. One was Mitch's little brother, Matthew. He was so excited, he was stammering.

"Something . . . something . . . something, *something* is wrong with the potty!" Matthew said. "A ghost! *Noises!*"

The kid beside him nodded furiously. His face was red, and he was out of breath.

Dad and I didn't even have to speak. We just sidestepped the kids and sprinted.

The kids were right. The Porta Potty on the far end was shaking and hollering like it was possessed!

In our family it's my mom the cop who's the brave one. But that day Dad didn't hesitate an instant. He ran up the two steps to the door, ripped it open, stood back, and—what do you know—out of there, almost knocking my dad over, wearing Uncle Sam–striped pants, a red-white-and-blue tailcoat, and star-spangled bicycle shoes, blasted Coach Banner!

He looked crazy. *What happened? How'd I get here? The run . . . the game?*

"Steady there, Sam, steady." Dad put a hand on Coach Banner's shoulder. "You're okay now. You're gonna be okay."

"Well, of course, I'm okay," Coach Banner snapped. "Except for a headache, and . . . why's the sun so low?" He put his hand to his forehead and frowned, then he staggered a step. "Now you mention it, I—" His knees buckled.

My dad grabbed one elbow, and I got the other. Together we helped him past the murmuring, awestruck little kids and over to the swings; then we eased him down into one. He clutched the chains to keep his balance. His eyes looked like they couldn't quite focus.

"Alex?" Coach Banner squinted up at me.

"Yeah, Coach?"

"Alex," he said slowly, "I can't be sure. But I *think* something very strange is going on."

Chapter Ten

It wasn't long before Mrs. Banner was beside us, tears running down her face.

"Oh, thank goodness, Sam! We were all so worried!"

She knelt next to her husband, who was still sitting in the swing, and put her arms around him. Poor Coach Banner was already confused, and now he was embarrassed, too.

Of course, by now everyone who had been at the game was alerted to the miracle of the Porta Potty, and a lot of people—including my mom—were crowding around, all happy Coach Banner was safe and in one piece.

"We'll have some questions, Sam," Mom told him. "But for now let's get you checked out by the medicos, see if they can figure out what happened."

"Won't be necessary," Coach Banner said. "I'm *fine*." But as soon as the words were out, he had a coughing fit.

"He *hates* doctors," Mrs. Banner said loudly so she could be heard over the coughing. "Are you sure it's necessary?"

Mom looked Mrs. Banner in the eye and nodded. "I'm sure."

Yasmeen was standing next to me, with Jeremiah beside her. Josh Banner had come over, too, but he was staying in the background, letting his mom do the huggy stuff. I caught his eye, and he tried to shrug like, *yeah, whatever*; but he was smiling. I think sometimes when a kid acts like he hates his parents, it's more for show than for real.

"We were looking in the wrong Porta Potties all along," Yasmeen said to me.

I scratched my head. "I know. But how could that be, anyway? The beard and the hat were on that tree across the park."

"It's like a magic trick," Yasmeen said. "Somebody goes in one box, the magician waves a wand, and he reappears in a different box."

"I guess," I said, "but who's the magician?"

Before we could ponder that anymore, I heard a siren; and then an ambulance sped into the parking lot and braked so fast the wheels spattered gravel.

So with an audience of all the baseball fans and parents, not to mention our team and even some of the players for Belletoona Pets & Fish, Coach Banner was laid out on a stretcher.

"I know how much he doesn't like this," I said to Yasmeen. "He wants everybody to think he's so totally tough."

The guys hauled the stretcher to the ambulance and started maneuvering it inside. Just before he disappeared Coach Banner raised a hand and held up two fingers—*V* for victory.

The crowd cheered. The siren revved up. The ambulance pulled away.

Everyone pretty much went home after the ambulance left, which meant the concession stand didn't do as much business as usual, and there were a lot of leftover hamburgers. Dad said he might as well grill them at home, so we had a cookout in the backyard for dinner. Mom was even there. Officer Krichels had agreed to work on the investigation so she could be home with

Dad and me and Luau. Dad and I did the dishes. Then I thought I'd get in a few games of Lousy Luigi before bed, but I was rudely interrupted by Mom, coming up the stairs from the basement.

"Alex, weren't you supposed to change Luau's litter box?" she asked.

"I'll do it tomorrow," I said. "I promise."

"That's what you said Friday," Mom said. "And Saturday. And yesterday. It's getting smelly down there."

"Okay, Mom. You don't have to be gross," I said.

We keep Luau's litter box in a corner in the laundry room. Every day—at least every day that I think of it—I clean out the lumps with a sifter scoop. Once a week I change the whole thing.

That night Luau followed me down the basement stairs. I took a deep breath and held it as I picked up the litter box and walked it to the outdoor trash to dump it. All the time Luau followed right along behind me, which was not usual.

"What's with you?" I asked. He didn't answer.

Going back into the laundry room, I put the empty box down so I could open the door. When I did Luau jumped in.

"What the . . . ?" I said. "Do you really have to go, or what? I'll be done in a second!" I tried to tip him out of the box, but he sat himself down and stayed put. So I lifted him and the box up and carried them both back to the corner.

"Oh, I get it," I laughed. "This is like a Porta Potty, right?"

Luau said mrrf, which meant *exactly*.

I set cat and box down, tickled Luau under the chin, and went to the cupboard for the bag of kitty litter. Then I went to the recycling box for some newspaper to line the box with. The sports section was on top, and I noticed a headline about Pennsylvania Youth Baseball, something to do with a new league getting started. Hey—maybe it was about that thing the guys saw on ESPN, so I put it aside and used the classified section instead. Then I poured in fresh litter.

"There. All yours," I said to Luau, who bumped my leg with his head to say thank you. I washed my hands in the laundry sink, picked up the paper I wanted to read, and carried it up the stairs. Luau surprised me again by following along behind. "I thought you had to go," I said.

On the sofa in the family room, I looked at the sports section I had rescued from a fate worse than recycling. The headline said: YOUTH BASEBALL TO TURN PRO?

COLLEGE SPRINGS—*A proposal for a nationwide baseball league that could pay salaries to players as young as 10 has Pennsylvania Youth Baseball fans and parents sharply divided.*

The idea is being floated by Nevada entrepreneur Louis Wynne. Reached at his offices in Sparks, Nev., Wynne acknowledged that he is in preliminary discussions with coaches and youth organizers in a number of states, as well as with potential financial backers.

"I've also been traveling around the country attending baseball games, and let me tell you, some of these kids I've seen-are great little athletes—a pleasure to watch," he said. "What's more American than heading to the ballpark on a Saturday afternoon to see the kids play ball? And what's more fun? And where there's fun, a guy like me sees the potential for profit."

Wynne likewise acknowledged that a potential source of funding for the new league is the gaming industry, which could reap big bucks from legalized gambling on youth teams. College and professional sports now attract bets totaling billions of dollars a year, he noted, and youth sports opens a whole new avenue of opportunity.

Rodney Shadle, president of the Middle County section of Pennsylvania Youth Baseball, would neither confirm nor deny reports that he and Wynne have had discussions. Shadle did say, however, that paying young athletes for their time is "not necessarily a bad idea in the current business and cultural climate."

Shadle, a former pitcher in the Pirates organization, went on to say, "Young athletes are essentially in the entertainment industry. We pay singers or actors regardless of their age—why not baseball stars?"

At least some parents agree. One baseball mom, who didn't want her name used, pointed out that there is big moneymaking potential in young talent, and that this potential should be exploited for the benefit of players and their families.

"Like it or not," she said, "that's capitalism. People are willing to pay top dollar for certain products. In this case the product is the spectacle of athletic talent."

She noted that unpaid college athletes have for years been making big bucks for universities and that this is "the height of exploitation."

But not all local coaches and parents believe that kids should be paid to play baseball.

Take teacher *Jean Muriel*, whose son plays first base on a Belletoona team.

"Kids should be kids," she said, "out for fun. They shouldn't feel the responsibility, the stress, of playing for money. If my son Brody had to worry about making the team and bringing in an income, he'd have an ulcer!"

And a youth coach who did not want his name used called the idea of paying young players "un-American," adding that kids should play sports as a means of learning traditional values.

"Sports should be about all that's good in America—camaraderie, excellence through hard work, fair play, grace under pressure. Instead, at the professional level these days, sports are mostly about greed and big egos. I would hate to see that kind of corruption pervade the youth level, too."

I read the article fast, then reread the beginning. That guy, Louis Wynne—he had been going to baseball games around the country—*and* he had talked to Rod Shadle right here in College Springs. I could be wrong, but didn't it seem possible that he had been here? That he had even come to a game here?

And then I remembered that guy I'd seen at some of our games lately, the one who dressed in Easter-egg colors. I had never seen a rich guy from Nevada before, not as far as I knew anyway; but didn't it seem likely that one would dress flashy like that? I would bet anything that it was Louis Wynne I'd been seeing at my games, that he was scouting for his new professional team!

I quickly thought back to how I had played today—a good catch at first and a solid hit in the fifth. Maybe if this new league deal worked out, I could get paid to play next season! How cool would that be?!

I was considering what video games my first earnings might buy when the phone rang. It was Yasmeen.

"I can't stop thinking about the case," she said. "You too?"

"What case?" I asked.

"Oh, come off it, Alex. I know you say you don't want to investigate, but you have to be thinking about it! Coach Banner goes in one Porta Potty and comes out another one. It's totally mysterious!"

"Oh, yeah, the kidnapping," I said. "But hey, Yasmeen, do you want to know something awesome?" And I told her what the article in the sports section had said.

Yasmeen said she hoped I'd remember my old friends when I was signing autographs and starring in commercials for bubblegum and body spray.

"I'll let you share my limo any time you want," I said. "My limo is your limo."

"Thanks, bud," she said. "But there's one other thing I don't get."

"What?" I said.

"Why would somebody go into a Porta Potty and fall asleep?"

Sometimes Yasmeen is too fast for me. "Huh? We are talking about my professional baseball career."

"I know that," she said. "But baseball makes me think of Coach Banner, and then I'm right back to thinking about the case. I mean, of course we're *not* investigating—because we agreed. But why did he fall asleep?"

"Who says he was asleep?"

"You saw him when he came out, Alex. Didn't he look confused—the way somebody does who's just waking up?"

I thought about that. "He did," I agreed. "And that would explain part of what happened. He couldn't escape from the Porta Potty on his own until he woke up."

"Exactly," Yasmeen said. "But why?"

"I don't know," I said. "Maybe the smell was so bad it knocked him out? Or maybe it's the chemicals they use in a Porta Potty? Maybe he's allergic to them. Maybe he had some kind of sleep reaction."

I thought these were pretty smart guesses, but Yasmeen said, "If Coach Banner were allergic to those chemicals, he'd fall asleep every time he went into a Porta Potty!"

I don't think I've ever met anyone as annoying as Yasmeen.

"*Fine*," I said. "It wasn't the chemicals at all. And besides, it doesn't matter. We are not going to investigate this case."

Chapter Eleven

As Bub would say, Let me amend that statement.

Tuesday Yasmeen called to tell me about a letter that came to her house in the mail, a letter addressed to "Kid Sleuths."

This is what it said:

> *Dear Sleuths,*
> *This is a ransom note. Follow its instructions to the letter and "Uncle" Sam Banner will be released unharmed.*
> *I do not want money. I want environmental action to save the Chesapeake Bay watershed. Please instruct Marguerite Banner that she must cease manufacturing and applying Uncle Sam's Lawn Care's patented Red-White-*

and-Blue formula because it contains pesti-cides and herbicides that are dangerous to the clams that rely on the ecosystem of the Chesa-peake Bay.

I am writing to you because of your reputation as detectives and because I believe you may have some influence with the Banner family. Remember: "Uncle" Sam Banner will not be returned to his wife and son until Marguerite Banner shuts down her business.

Yours very sincerely,
The Kidnapper
On behalf of the Friends of the Clams

I read this over sitting at Yasmeen's kitchen table. Her dad and mom were still at work, so she was in charge of Jeremiah. The letter surprised me so much I couldn't even talk. I just kept staring at it. Finally I said, "But Sam Banner has already been released!"

Yasmeen is African-American, so she never goes what you'd call pale; but if she did, she would have been looking pale that day.

"Is he okay?" Yasmeen asked.

"He's fine," I said. "My mom's been out to his house today. She said he's planning to go back to work." I reached across the table. "Let me see the envelope."

Yasmeen handed it over. "Kid Sleuths" and Yasmeen's address were printed in regular print on a white computer label. No return address. The postmark had the College Springs zip code, with Saturday's date.

Wait a second—postmarked Saturday?

"Yasmeen, this was mailed before Coach Banner was even kidnapped!" I said.

"I'm way ahead of you, bud," she said. "As usual. The question is, What does it mean?"

I ignored her "as usual" comment. "I have no idea what it means," I said, "but I do have a plan. We take this letter, walk next door, hand it to my mom—and forget we ever saw it."

"We can't do that!" Yasmeen argued. "Now we're part of the case whether we want to be or not."

"Not me."

Yasmeen sighed. "Okay. We'll take it to your mom. But . . . what if first we Google the clam people. That's not really investigating. It's just research."

I guessed there was nothing really wrong with a quick Google. So we went into her parents' office and sat down at the computer. Yasmeen typed in F-r-i-e-n-d-s o-f t-h-e C-l-a-m-s. The computer shot back Friends of the Earth and a lot of clam chowder recipes, but no exact match.

"That's weird," Yasmeen said. "Usually everybody has a website—even my grandma and Jeremiah's tae kwon do team. If there's no website, it's like Friends of the Clam doesn't really exist."

Chapter Twelve

Five minutes later Jeremiah, Yasmeen, and I were in the family room at my house with my mom and Luau. As soon as I sat down, Luau jumped in my lap and made a big to-do out of arranging himself. Jeremiah sat on the floor with the sports section and a calculator so he could study box scores and figure out player statistics. I don't think Yasmeen's idea that baseball would make him less weird was exactly working out.

Mom read the ransom letter twice. Then she put it in a special clear bag that's used for evidence and set it down on the coffee table.

"It looks like the kidnapper wants you two involved in solving this crime," she said.

"Well the kidnapper will sure be disappointed then," I said.

"But if the police need us, Alex," Yasmeen said. "We have to do our civic duty."

"I think we at the PD can handle it," Mom said. She sounded annoyed. But then she slumped back in her chair and smiled. "Sorry, honey. Today has been particularly trying."

"How come?" I asked.

Mom closed her eyes and took a breath, but when she spoke she didn't answer the question. "The obvious conclusion is that something knocked poor Coach Banner out yesterday. Wouldn't you say so?"

Yasmeen leaned forward. "That's what we think, too. But he didn't have any bruises or anything, right? It's not like he was hit on the head."

"The hospital said he checked out clean for physical trauma," Mom said. "So it must have been something else that knocked him out."

"An injection?" I said.

Mom nodded. "Possible. But then there'd be a puncture mark somewhere—plus the kidnapper would have had to get close enough to administer it—and all without attracting suspicion."

"Something he ate?" Yasmeen said.

"Or drank," I added. "Everybody's got a water bottle. Maybe there was something in his water."

"Also possible," Mom said. "But the kidnapper would have to be sure Coach Banner drank it at precisely the right time. Otherwise he might have passed out before he got to the Porta Potty."

"A gas!" Yasmeen said.

Mom nodded. "Bingo," she said. "In an enclosed space like that, it seems the most likely. It could have been deployed when he opened and closed the door to the Porta Potty—some kind of trip mechanism on a gas canister. That way the kidnapper would be sure the victim passed out when he was hidden away inside."

"But what if somebody else had used the Porta Potty first?" I asked.

Mom nodded. "A problem. But maybe the kidnapper was watching from a distance? Maybe the kidnapper had some kind of remote-control device?"

"You're a genius, Mom!" I said.

Mom laughed. "Thanks, honey. At least maybe I'm as smart as your basic ecoterrorist kidnapper."

Jeremiah was punching buttons on the calculator. But he hates it when he doesn't know something, and now he looked up. "What's *ecoterrorist?*"

Yasmeen kicked into dictionary mode. "An ecoterrorist is a person who believes that violence is justified to protect the environment."

"Like your letter writer," Mom said. "Apparently he thought kidnapping Uncle Sam would help save Chesapeake Bay from dangerous lawn chemicals."

I realized for the first time I didn't really understand that. "What do lawn chemicals in Pennsylvania have to do with the Chesapeake Bay? The bay's not even in Pennsylvania."

Yasmeen knew all about it, of course. "The Chesapeake Bay is in Maryland and Virginia," she said. Then she explained that anything you put on your grass eventually filters into the groundwater, and from there it seeps into creeks, streams, and rivers. In our part of Pennsylvania, the main river is the Susquehanna, and it drains all the way down into the Chesapeake Bay. A chemical that's good for making your lawn green might be poison to fish, or poison to the plants fish eat, or poison to clams.

"So whoever wrote the letter believes that Red-White-and-Blue formula is getting into the river, then to the bay, and hurting the clams," Yasmeen said.

"But is that true?" I asked.

"Maybe," Mom said. But then she added that the government has tons of rules regulating chemicals like pesticides, and anyone violating those rules would get in trouble with the government.

We were all quiet for a few seconds, thinking. Then I remembered how Mom said her day had been tough, but she still hadn't told us why. "What was so 'trying' about your day, Mom?" I asked her.

Mom shook her head and scrunched up her eyes like she was remembering a bad taste. "Fred Krichels," she said.

"Not again," Yasmeen said.

"Oh, I shouldn't complain," Mom said. "He tries hard and he means well, but sometimes . . . "

"What'd he do?" I asked.

"Let's say it *was* a gas that knocked out Uncle Sam," Mom began. "Chances are there'd be some residue in his clothing. There might be anyway. But I took the holiday off, and Fred didn't think to take the clothes as evidence. If we had them we could have sent them to the state lab. Then—maybe—we'd find out what it was that knocked Sam Banner out. If it was something unusual. . . ."

"But you were at his house today," I said. "Couldn't you pick up the clothes then?"

"Maggie Banner—I mean *Marguerite*—met me at the door with a laundry basket in her hand," Mom said. "She had already washed everything: the Uncle Sam coat, the sweats he was wearing before—even his underwear. That woman is too efficient."

"What about the lab tests at the hospital?" Yasmeen asked. "Coach Banner's blood and, uh . . . other fluids?"

Mom smiled. "You *are* a smart one, Yasmeen," she said. "And you're right. But the preliminary reports on the blood from the hospital's own lab are inconclusive. And since Coach Banner's home safe and sound, the case is kind of on the back burner."

"What about the hat?" Yasmeen asked. "Mrs. Banner wouldn't have washed the hat."

"It wasn't with him, remember?" I said. "Bub wore it for the parade. Did you interrogate Coach Banner, Mom?"

"I interviewed him," she said. "He remembers talking to you and Bub before the race, and hanging his hat and beard on the tree limb. He figures he must have gone into the Porta Potty closest to the tree to change. That's what he was planning to do. But he doesn't actually remember doing it."

"So maybe he went to the other Porta Potties after all," I said.

Mom nodded. "Maybe," she said. "Only everyone agrees there were a lot of runners around those Porta Potties before the race."

"I don't get it," Yasmeen said. "Why wouldn't Coach Banner remember what happened?"

"It happens to accident victims, too," Mom said. "A doctor explained it to me once. Your brain is more like a DVD player than a VCR. If you stop it and try to go back, you skip to the beginning of the scene—not the exact place you left off. Anyway it looks like his brain suffered some kind of disturbance."

"Does he remember the explosion and the fireworks?" I asked.

"No," Mom said. "He must've been out cold by then."

Yasmeen pulled a notebook out of her back pocket and started writing. I did not like the looks of that.

"What are you doing?" I asked.

She dropped the notebook into her lap. "If I

tell you what I'm writing, you'll only get mad. You don't want to be mad, so don't ask, okay?"

Mom laughed. "Are you writing down what we've got so far?" she asked.

Yasmeen nodded. "I can't help it. I'm going to be thinking about it anyway, so I might as well be organized."

"Tell me what you've got then," Mom said.

"The kidnapper is an ecoterrorist who was watching Coach Banner, waiting for him to go into the Porta Potty. The ecoterrorist tripped some kind of device that sent gas into the Porta Potty, the gas put Coach Banner to sleep. Later he woke up and started yelling," Yasmeen said.

"And the letter?" Mom asked.

"It looks like the kidnapper meant to keep him for a while," I said, forgetting I wasn't investigating.

"Something must have gone wrong," Yasmeen said thoughtfully. "But what?"

I thought back to that morning, and the answer was obvious. "The explosion," I said.

Yasmeen and Mom both looked at me. Usually when they look at me like that, they're about to tell me that I'm pretty dumb for a smart kid, but not this time. "Of course!" they said almost like a chorus.

"With fire guys and police all over the park, the kidnapper couldn't take Coach Banner away like he planned to," Yasmeen said.

"But aren't we forgetting one thing?" Mom asked. As she spoke Luau jumped up onto the back of the sofa, said a quick sharp *meow*, stretched, and swished his tail.

I reached over my shoulder to pat my cat. "What?" I asked Mom.

It was Yasmeen who answered. "The magic trick." She scribbled in her notebook. "Coach Banner went in one Porta Potty and came out the other."

Sometimes Luau seems to be following people conversations and sometimes not. Right then I had the feeling he was listening to what we were saying and even trying to make a comment of his own. Only I couldn't figure out what he was getting at. It was like last night when he made his own Porta Potty out of the litter box—jumped in it so I'd have to carry him. Now he put his front paws on my shoulder and blurted another meow, *Think, Alex!*—and then I saw it.

"You're a genius!" I said to my cat.

Yasmeen rolled her eyes. It doesn't matter how many times I explain to Yasmeen about communicating with Luau, she refuses to get it. "Oh not this cat-conversation stuff again," she said. "Okay, Alex, go ahead and tell us. What is it you think your cat's talking about now?"

I was too excited to let sarcasm bother me. "Porta Potties are, uh . . . portable, right?" I said. "So what if it wasn't just Coach Banner who moved? What if it was the whole Porta Potty—with him in it?"

Yasmeen shook her head. "If a Porta Potty was missing from one place, and there was an extra in another place . . . we would've noticed."

"How many Porta Potties were on the alley side of the park?" I asked her. "How many were by the playground?"

"Uh . . ." For once Yasmeen was at a loss for words.

"See?" I said. "You don't remember, and neither do I. There were two rows of them—maybe five, maybe six—even seven?" I said. "I think somebody could have moved one, and in all the excitement, nobody paid attention. Who counts Porta Potties?"

Jeremiah sang under his breath, "One little, two little, three little Porta Potties . . ." This, as far as I know, is the only joke Jeremiah has ever made in his life. We all cracked up—even Jeremiah.

Then I asked my mom, "What do you think?"

She nodded. "There's a chance—a slight chance—you're right," she said.

"I can call the company if you want," Yasmeen said. "They must keep track of their own Porta Potties."

"Oh, no," I said, "you are not calling the company. Because that would be investigating. And we don't have time to investigate. I mean, I haven't even *started* the Decades Project yet."

My mom's eyebrows shot up.

Jeremiah said, "Uh-oh."

"What do you *mean* you haven't started?" my mom said. "You've had that assignment for two weeks, Alex Parakeet!"

I studied my shoelaces. They were clean and white. "I know, Mom."

"And you *told* me you were working on it!"

"I *was*," I said. "Sort of. I mean I was working on getting *started* on working on it."

Jeremiah hummed the first few notes of the funeral march. "Dum-dum-de-dum-DUM-de-dum-dum-dum-dum-DUM," and Yasmeen squashed her lips together the way you do when you're trying not to laugh.

The phone was on the table next to the sofa.

Mom got up, went over to it, and handed it to me. "Didn't you say you're going to interview Bub? Call him this instant and set that up for tomorrow."

I didn't know which was worse, being embarrassed in front of my friends or actually having to start the assignment. But I dialed, hoping Bub wouldn't be home.

He answered on the first ring.

And worse yet he told me tomorrow would be just fine. He would show me his old Air Force uniform. And he'd have a big bowl of mushroom soup waiting for me.

I *hate* mushroom soup.

Chapter Thirteen

The idea of the Decades Project is you get assigned a decade of the twentieth century, and you have to do a presentation for the class on everything about it—clothes, music, politics, movies. If you get a recent enough decade, it's a good idea to interview somebody about what it was like to live then. My decade was the 1960s, right before my parents were born, so my mom and dad suggested I talk to Bub. One of the big things that happened in the 1960s was the Vietnam War, and Bub was there.

At lunch at school the next day, Yasmeen pulled out her notes on the Uncle Sam case.

"Be sure to ask your mom about the Porta

Potties," she said. We were sitting at our favorite table in the caf. Nobody had sat down with us yet.

"I will not," I said.

"Then I'll talk to her myself."

"You can't do that!" I said.

"Why not?" Yasmeen asked.

I was going to tell her—*because we're not detecting, remember?*—but Ashley and Teresa came over with their lunch trays and sat down. They both had strawberry milk, giant cookies, and pink Jell-O.

"Can we sit with the celebrity couple?" Ashley asked. Teresa giggled.

Yasmeen frowned and took a big bite of the bologna sandwich she had brought from home.

"Or maybe Yasmeen thinks she's too good for us," Teresa said.

I thought Yasmeen would ignore that, too, but she snapped, "At least I've got something to think about besides what flavor lip gloss to wear."

"Yasmeen!" I said.

"That's okay, Alex," Ashley said. "We know we're not as smart as Yasmeen is."

"Nobody's as smart as she is. Or as stuck-up, either," Teresa said.

I couldn't believe it. What is with girls anyway?

I was afraid I was about to witness all-out war. But luckily Ari came over with his tray and asked if anybody had the homework. Then some other kids sat down. Yasmeen didn't say another word the rest of lunch, and I didn't see her after school because on Wednesday her dad picks her up for piano lessons.

When I got to Bub's, Dad was visiting, and so was Luau. Sometimes Bub's is like the neighborhood hangout.

I didn't know how to reject the bowl of mushroom soup without being rude, so I said thank you and took a tiny sip.

"Have you got your notebook?" Dad asked me.

"Yeah," I said after I had tried another sip, "but I've been thinking about it and I thought maybe it would be a better idea to interview Bub tomorrow after I do some research on the computer first. Also I don't have a camera to take a picture of the uniform."

Dad was sitting in a chair across from me at the table. As usual Bub was at the head, and Luau was in the big stuffed chair, watching TV with the sound off.

Dad reached under his chair. "Guess what I

brought from home," he said. And there, unfortunately, was the digital camera. "You know, Alex, starting a project is always the hardest part. You'll feel less stressed once you've gotten going."

"I'm not the one who's stressed!" I said. "Mom is! I always get my projects done . . . eventually."

Dad raised his eyebrows. "It seems to me sometimes there's a pretty big panic the night before the due date."

I harrumphed and concentrated on my soup, which wasn't as bad as I expected, even if it was gray, which is not a natural color for food.

Bub said, "Mushroom is not in my usual, whatchacall, repertoire. I only made it today because Jo brought over the mushrooms." Jo is Bub's niece who goes to college. "She's got a roommate studying mycology—everything a person can possibly know about mushrooms. These were organic," Bub went on, "left over from a project o' hers."

"Organic" reminded me of the ransom note, so while Dad brought me more soup, I filled Bub in on the latest with the Uncle Sam mystery.

"That's a puzzler for sure," Bub said. "Are you and Yasmeen gonna work on it?"

"No way!" I said.

The three of us talked about the mystery without getting anywhere, and we talked about Jo. Bub told me mushrooms aren't the only unusual thing you can study up at the college. You can study hospitality management, which is a fancy way of saying how to work in a hotel or a restaurant; and turf management, which is a fancy way of saying lawn care. Dad said Coach Banner used to be a professor of turf management before he quit to help Mrs. Banner start Uncle Sam's Lawn Care.

"Was Mrs. Banner a turf management professor, too?" I asked. "Before she invented Red-White-and-Blue formula?"

"Biochemistry, I think," Dad said. "Or molecular biology? Anyway—now I need to get home and finish up my chores. Coming, Luau?"

Luau didn't even look up. He was glued to a cat food commercial, starring a big white Persian in a pink jeweled collar.

"Guess not," Dad said. Then he turned to me. "Take your time with the interview," he said. "Dinner's not till seven. You won't be hungry till then anyway."

When Dad left, Bub went and retrieved his old Air Force uniform, which he kept in a box under his bed. Bub set the box on the table and opened it. There was a sharp smell, clean and toxic at the same time. Bub pulled out a dark blue jacket, dark blue trousers, and a pale blue button-up shirt. On the jacket were colorful pins that Bub said were called campaign ribbons, even though they didn't look like any ribbons I had ever seen.

The most amazing thing about the uniform was how skinny it was. It would've taken two to fit around the Bub I knew.

Bub must've been thinking the same thing because he said, "Guess I've eaten more'n my share o' soup since those days, huh?"

There are no good answers to some questions, and this was one. I half shrugged and half smiled, and went ahead and snapped a couple of pictures. Then I said, "Tell me about Vietnam. What was the best part?"

Bub looked surprised, like that was a question he didn't expect. "Well, I guess it was the other guys, my buddies," he said. "You got to depend on each other in a way that doesn't happen much except in war—life or death, so you get close."

I wrote this down, thinking the interview thing was going to be easy. I was practically done already.

But then Bub said, "Were you going to ask me

the worst thing, too? Because that's an easy one. When the war was finally over—in 1975—almost sixty thousand American soldiers were dead, not to mention thousands more Vietnamese people; and the North Vietnamese—the Communists— got the country after all." Bub shook his head. "And now we trade with them—with the enemy that whupped us—just like they were anybody else. Did you know a lot of the shrimp you buy at the supermarket come from Vietnam?"

I shook my head.

Bub looked down at his lap, then back up at me. "It's a crazy world," he said finally. Then, "Hey!" He pointed at my notebook. "Why aren't you writing this down?"

"Oh, I forgot," I said. *Crazy world*, I wrote; *60,000*. Was this what Mrs. Weaver wanted?

"What was America like back then?" I asked. "When you got back from being in the Air Force, I mean."

"I served in '66–67," Bub said. "So things weren't too bad yet."

Now I was surprised. "Bad?"

"I mean, the antiwar protests hadn't gotten too bad."

I didn't know what he was talking about, so he

explained that the war became unpopular in the United States, and a lot of people protested against it. There were marches in the streets and something called sit-ins.

"When I came home in '67, I couldn't believe how much the country had changed," Bub said. "It seemed like all of a sudden people who used to be normal had grown their hair long and were wearing tie-dyed T-shirts and flashing the peace sign. A bunch o' hippies!"

"What *is* a hippie?" I asked. "I mean, besides an easy Halloween costume."

Bub laughed. "You know your baseball coach? Hathaway? Now there's a hippie."

"How do you know Coach Hathaway?"

"It's a small town," Bub said. "He and I are about the same age, and he served in Vietnam, too. But when he came back, he joined the peace movement, grew his hair long, went back to school. I kept my hair short, quit school, and got a job at a coal mine, same as my dad and my uncles. Hey— you stopped taking notes again."

Oh, shoot. *Tie-dye. Long hair. Hippies. Coal mine.*

Bub started twiddling his thumbs the way he does when he's thinking. "You asked what a hippie is," he went on, watching his thumbs. "The long hair was just what you might call a label. Being a hippie meant having certain beliefs, too—a way of looking at life. Your hippies—they believed in peace and love and rock 'n' roll."

I thought about that a minute, then I said, "Sounds good."

Bub laughed, and this time his whole body shook, especially his big belly. "All right, smarty-pants," he said. "I guess I like all those things, too. But the difference between me and the hippies is *I* know they're not enough. *I* know you can't have peace and love—or even rock 'n' roll—if you're not safe from your enemies. And one thing about your enemies, Alex, you can't count on 'em to be sweet as pie."

"But I don't get it," I said. "Are you telling me Coach Hathaway doesn't believe in being safe?"

"Not safe enough in my opinion," Bub said. "But maybe you oughta ask *him*." He nodded at my notebook again, and I wrote *peace, love, sweet as pie*. Meanwhile in the recliner Luau got up and stretched, then jumped down, and padded over to rub against my leg.

"Getting to be time for his dinner, I bet," Bub said.

I was still writing. "He doesn't eat till six."

"Well it's after that now," Bub said.

I couldn't believe it. Was it possible we had been talking that long? I ran my hand along Luau's backbone. "Poor starving guy." Then I started gathering up my stuff—backpack, notebook, camera.

Bub folded his hands across his belly. "Me personally, I think I'll skip dinner."

"Why?"

Bub glanced right and left like someone might overhear, then he cupped his hands around his mouth. "Diet."

"Okay, but why are you whispering?" I asked.

"Bad luck if you don't," he said. "I read it at the barbershop. If you go on a"—he lowered his voice—"*diet* . . . and you tell everybody about it, it doesn't work. This has been scientifically studied."

"When Mom goes on a diet, she gets grumpy," I said.

Bub leaned back in his chair and smiled. "For me that won't be a problem. I'm grumpy as a body can be already."

Chapter Fourteen

Dinner was shrimp stir-fry with ginger and garlic. When I smelled it on the stove, I thought back to the good old days before Dad got into cooking— when we ate stuff like boxed mac 'n' cheese. Now you never knew what you might get for dinner. Nothing normal, that was for sure.

"Did these shrimp come from Vietnam?" I asked when we were all sitting at the table.

"The passports weren't in the package," Dad said. "Does it matter?"

I picked at my rice and told Mom and Dad about my interview with Bub, what he said about "the enemy."

"I disagree with Bub," Mom said. "We buy Japanese cars, too, even though we fought Japan in World War II. I think the more we buy stuff from other countries, the more we have to get along, and the more peaceful the world is."

"I don't think that's what Bub—" I started to say, but some commotion coming from the front door stopped me. It sounded like maybe the door was being hacked into kindling.

I could see Mom and Dad were alarmed, but not me. There is only one person capable of making that much noise just walking into a house, and most of the time she's not dangerous. So I took advantage of Mom's and Dad's distraction to knock a couple of my shrimps onto the floor for Luau. Five seconds later, just as I expected, Sofie Sikora barreled into the kitchen.

"Hi!" she said.

My mom is not Sofie's number one fan. Right now her hand was over her heart, and she was taking a deep breath. "You scared me to death!" she said. "Have you ever heard of a doorbell?"

"Sure!" Sofie said. "I fix doorbells! Maybe yours is busted. That happens a lot, you know. If it is, it costs ten dollars to have me fix it. Or maybe I didn't ring it. I don't remember. Oh—you're eating dinner! Is there food left or some cereal? Because at our house we had a really bad dinner.

My mom got Chinese from the new place and she let Byron pick and he picked tofu, which is the same as having pieces of sponge in your food if you didn't know, plus there was some kind of green stuff on it. The rice was okay because I made my mom put butter—"

"Sofie?" My dad interrupted. He knows if you don't interrupt Sofie, there's the totally real possibility she will talk forever.

Sofie kept talking for a few more seconds like a car that keeps moving after you hit the brakes. But then she paused and said, "Yes, Mr. Parakeet?"

"There's some shrimp left if you'd like that. I'm sorry, but I neglected to ask where it was born."

Sofie's face twisted in disgust. "*Ewwww!*" she said. "How can you eat that stuff? No offense, Luau," she added. Luau had a shrimp dangling from his mouth.

"How about a nice bowl of Pirate Berry Crunch?" Dad asked.

"That would be delicious, thank you, Mr. Parakeet," Sofie said; and she dropped down in the chair next to me, expecting her bowl of cereal to be delivered. Once Dad told me he gets a kick out of Sofie. He says it's better to get a kick out of her than to let her raise your blood pressure like Mom does. A couple of minutes later, he presented Sofie with her cereal.

"Do you have strawberry milk?" Sofie asked.

"We have white," my mom said. She was not smiling.

"White's okay," Sofie said.

Dad delivered Sofie's milk, then raised his eyebrows and nodded at me, which meant I should clear his and Mom's and my dishes. I didn't see why I had to work like a servant when Sofie was treated like a queen, but Mom was already in a bad mood, so I didn't argue.

"What brings you over here, Sofie?" my dad asked.

There was a pause while she tried to remember. Then she said, "Oh!" and she started feeling around in the back pocket of her jeans. Finally she yanked out a limp, crumpled piece of paper. "My mom sent me. It's this form for the school picnic. You're in charge of the forms, aren't you, Mr. Parakeet? My mom said they put *you* in charge because all the moms are too busy. She says it would be better if you went back to work so your family could afford a nicer car because yours is an eyesore. Hey—maybe if you went back to work,

Mr. Parakeet, you could afford strawberry milk instead of only plain white. My mom says—"

"I'll take the form, Sofie," Mom said. "Would you like some more cereal? Poor as we are, we can still afford that."

Before she finally left Sofie ate another bowl of cereal and asked for a third, but that was the end of the box. While I loaded the dishwasher, Dad wrote out a shopping list; then he left for the grocery store so we'd have enough cereal and milk for breakfast. Mom and I went into the family room. She plopped down into the recliner to read the newspaper. I got on the computer so I could type some notes about what Bub said. I had been planning to put that off, but with Mom right there, I couldn't exactly play Lousy Luigi.

I was almost done with my notes when Mom let the newspaper fall into her lap and looked up at me. "You're planning to talk to Coach Hathaway, too, right?" she asked.

I didn't want Mom to get the idea nagging is effective, so I avoided the question with a question of my own. "What's new with the Uncle Sam case? Did you call the Porta Potty company to see if one of 'em was moved?"

My strategy worked.

"They're inventorying today," Mom said. "I should know tomorrow. There *was* something new with the fire at the fireworks shed, though. The arson team's done with the on-scene part of their investigation. They think they've got an incendiary device."

"A what?"

"A thingy made to start a fire," Mom said.

"You're kidding," I said. "Why would anybody have wanted to start that fire on purpose?"

"Somebody who hates the Fourth of July?" Mom said. "Or . . . who knows? Anyway, arson investigators don't deal with why."

I thought for a minute. "What kind of an incen-di-ary device?"

Mom said pretty much all that was left was burned metal and traces of a chemical that could have started the fire. "But the arson guys think it was pretty sophisticated—something activated by a radio signal. It didn't need to be very powerful because it was in a shed full of fireworks. Just a flame, or even heat, and *kaboom*!"

A radio signal? "Wait a sec," I said. "You mean like a remote control?"

Mom nodded, but I could see from her face she didn't get it.

"Mom," I said, "didn't we say maybe if there was sleeping gas in the Porta Potty, it was released by remote control, too?"

Mom sat up. *Now* she was getting it. "Oh, my goodness, Alex! You're *right!*"

"If that's true," I said, thinking while I talked, "then it seems like the same person who knocked out Coach Banner and sent the ransom note also set the fire that blew up the shed. I mean, otherwise it's too big a coincidence, right? *Two* remote controls?"

Mom leaned back in her chair and stared at me for a second. "I don't know why I didn't realize that, Alex," she said. "I must be working too hard. Anyway—good for you, kid."

Someone else's mom might say "good for you" all the time—like when the kid just makes his bed or puts the cap back on the toothpaste. With my mom, "good for you" is like I set a Guinness record or won some international prize. It felt really good to hear it. "Thanks, Mom," I said.

Mom smiled. "And you know something else—what I want you to do for me right now?"

I smiled back. "What?"

"Call Coach Hathaway and set up a Decades Project interview for tomorrow after school."

Before I went to bed, I called Yasmeen. It was the first time I'd had a chance to talk to her since she had the argument with Ashley and Teresa at lunch, but I felt embarrassed about bringing it up. And anyway I had something more important to tell her—that the arson team had found part of a remote control in the fireworks shed.

"That means the explosion was a *whatchacallit*!" I said confidently.

"Diversion!" Yasmeen said. "While everybody was running toward the fire and the fireworks, the kidnapper was moving the Porta Potty with Coach Banner inside it."

"That's what I think, too," I said.

"So I guess we were wrong about one thing," Yasmeen went on. "The explosion didn't *thwart* the kidnapper's plan, it was *part* of the kidnapper's plan."

"But if that's true, why didn't the kidnapper actually *kidnap* Coach Banner? Why was he still stuck in the Porta Potty after the baseball game? The ransom note doesn't make any sense!"

"Maybe something else went wrong," Yasmeen said. "Maybe when we figure that out, we'll have solved the case."

"Except *we're* not solving the case," I said. "Remember?"

Chapter Fifteen

The next day after school, I rode my bike to the university campus to interview Coach Hathaway at his office in the Carnegie Building. It was easy to find because this time of year—when the college students had already gone home for summer break—it was the only faculty office with the door open.

I went in, and Coach Hathaway stood up to greet me.

"Alex!" He smiled and held out his hand. Along with his usual sweats, he was wearing a blue T-shirt. On the front were the words *Liberal? Or just well-educated?* I shook hands with him and looked around. There was a signed photograph of my dad's favorite baseball player, Roberto Clemente, hanging on the wall behind the desk. It was crooked. There were Christmas lights strung from a curtain rod with no curtains, and stacks of papers and books piled on the desk and the floor. Everything looked a little dusty. With his gray hair, so did Professor Hathaway.

"Clear some of that junk off the chair and have a seat," he told me. "You've got a school project, is that it?"

I explained. "And I already talked to Bub Wisniewski. He's my neighbor," I said.

"Sure, I know Bub." Coach Hathaway nodded. "He's a good guy—a bit misguided in his thinking, but a good guy. So what you want from me is the other side of the sixties, then? You know I was in 'Nam?"

I got out my notebook. "What did you do there?" I asked.

"I was a demolition guy—bombs, in other words," he said.

"Bombs?!" I said.

"War is ugly," he said, like that explained it. "Destructive. It meant a kind of ugliness a small-town boy from Pennsylvania never knew existed. And I don't mean just blood, either. I mean the way it got to our heads, to the GIs. We all got ugly, too—our attitudes about the enemy. It's a cliché to say life is cheap, but that's how it seemed. Don't let anybody tell you different, Alex. There is *nothing* glorious about war."

I realized my coach was talking like he'd said all this before. I guess that's how it is if you're a professor. You get paid to talk.

"Nothing glorious," I repeated, still writing.

"Well," he said, "maybe there is one thing. And that's the camaraderie. Do you know that word?"

"Like friends?" I asked.

"The bonds between friends. When your life depends on the guy next to you doing his job right, you develop a very special feeling for the guy next to you."

"You and Bub agree about that," I told him. "To me it sounds a little like baseball."

Coach Hathaway smiled. "That's a pretty good analogy. What else do you want to know about the war?"

"Bub said when he came home, a lot of people were protesting the war."

"True," Coach Hathaway said. "And by the time I got back, I didn't like the war any more than they did. So I joined them, became a protester."

"But I don't get it," I said. "Why had you joined up in the first place?"

"I joined up out of patriotism, same as Bub did," Coach Hathaway said. "I wanted to spread democracy. It may not be a perfect form of government, but it's the best one anybody's ever come up with. Then I got to Vietnam, and I couldn't see how shooting at people was doing anything to spread good government. And after I came back, I decided patriotism meant telling our own government the war was a mistake."

This made sense to me. But when I was talking to Bub, he made sense, too. This sixties decade sure was confusing.

"I read that some of the protesters broke the law," I said.

Coach Hathaway nodded. "They got carried away," he said. "There were bombings—bad stuff. I got arrested my fair share of times."

"*You* got arrested?" My hand was starting to hurt from all the writing I was doing.

"Sometimes you break a law to make a point. It's called civil disobedience. It gets people's attention. There's a long tradition of that in this country."

"Really?" I said. "I never heard of it."

Coach Hathaway was grinning. "I bet you did. How about a little fracas called the Boston Tea Party?"

Of course I remembered the Boston Tea Party from school. In 1773 some colonists who didn't like a new tax dressed up like Indians, climbed aboard an English ship in the harbor in Boston, and threw the cargo of tea into the water. "That was—whatever you said—civil disobedience?" I asked.

"A prime example. Vandalism, theft . . . How do you think the owner of the tea felt?"

I had never thought about the owner of the tea before.

"And what about Rosa Parks?" said Coach Hathaway. "It was illegal for her to sit down in that bus, too."

Because my mind was still on the case, I couldn't help thinking about the ransom letter Yasmeen and I got. The person who kidnapped Coach Banner said he did it to save the clams, right? Was the kidnapping supposed to be a case of civil disobedience?

I wanted to talk to Coach Hathaway about this, but it was almost time for baseball practice. And there was something else, too. Some little part of my brain told me to be careful how much I said to Coach Hathaway. After all he and Coach Banner didn't like each other—everybody knew that. Maybe Coach Hathaway didn't think it was totally a bad thing that Coach Banner got kidnapped. Maybe he thought the herbicides in Uncle Sam's Red-White-and-Blue formula were bad for the clams, too. Hadn't he just said he'd been arrested before?

"We better get," Coach Hathaway said. "I see you've brought your baseball bag. We can throw it and your bike in the back of my old truck. If you've got more questions, we'll talk on the way."

Coach Hathaway's truck was as messy as his office and almost as full of books. I had to clear a space for myself before I could sit down in the passenger seat, and I wound up with a pile of books in my lap. I noticed one of them had a funny name, *The Monkey Wrench Gang*. I wondered what that was about, but before I could ask, he started the truck and asked me if I thought the Pirates should go ahead and trade their best closer, and I said no way, and after that we talked about baseball all the way to practice.

* * *

Mom picked me up after baseball. We lugged my bike out of Coach Hathaway's truck and wrestled it into the back of the car. Then I climbed into the passenger seat.

"I've got good news about the case," Mom said as she backed out of the parking space. Once we were on the highway, she explained that Missy from Regular John had called her back, and it turned out one of the Porta Potties was moved across the park sometime between Thursday, when it was put in place, and Tuesday, when it was picked up for cleaning. "There's something else, too," Mom added. "On several of the Porta Potties, it looks like somebody fiddled with the latches."

"The latches?" I said. "You mean like the door handles?"

"Exactly," Mom said. "The door handles in the Porta Potties on the far side of the park had been twisted so the sign said 'occupied' even when they were unlocked."

I remembered noticing the "occupied" signs on the Porta Potties on Memorial Day. But I hadn't thought about it since. Now that I did, something else occured to me. "Wait a sec," I said. "Were they *all* twisted that way?"

Mom grinned. "Alex, you're a detective even when you don't want to be. Nope, not all. Guess which one *wasn't*."

"The one that was moved," I said.

"Bingo," Mom said. "That must be how our kidnapper guaranteed that Coach Banner would use that one particular Porta Potty, the one with the knockout gas ready inside."

"So if the kidnapper messed with the latches and all that, there must be fingerprints, right?"

Mom sighed. "We've been one step behind on everything in this case. We'll check, of course, but Regular John has already cleaned those boxes and swabbed them out. I doubt there's anything left for us to find."

"What are you going to do next?" I asked.

"We'll interview the neighbors," Mom said. "I'm not real optimistic. We talked to plenty of people that same afternoon, and not one mentioned migrating Porta Potties."

"So what do you do after you talk to the neighbors?" I asked.

Mom turned the car onto Chickadee Court. "Well, I've got one more avenue left to explore," she said. "But it's pretty unlikely we'll get anywhere with it, and it will take a lot of manpower to pull it off." She nodded at me, which was my signal to press the button on the garage-door opener. "Plus the chief told me today I need to focus my efforts on that, uh . . . the other project."

"The federal one?" I asked as we turned into the driveway and the garage door started to rise.

Mom smiled. "For now let's just say 'the other project.'" She pulled the car into the garage, stopped, and killed the engine. Mom sighed, and for a second neither of us moved. "With summer coming," she finally said, "and vacations, we're going to be short-staffed. And with Coach Banner safe and sound, his kidnapping isn't the priority. Some cases never get solved, and this could be one of those cases."

Chapter Sixteen

The last two weeks of school went by in a blur, and summer started at last. Here are some highlights:

1. Uncle Sam's Lawn Care lost its last regular-season game, 6–0. Coach Banner had an argument with Josh about his scruffy hair before the game, and Josh, as usual, only played one inning.

2. I got an A on the Decades Project. Mrs. Weaver liked my interviews with Bub and Coach Hathaway, and she loved the tie-dyed T-shirt and granny glasses I wore when I made my presentation.

3. Yasmeen's family left for the shore the way they always do at the start of vacation.

4. I got picked for the PYB Summer All-Star team. (Surprise!)

5. The PYB Middle County commissioners selected Sam Banner and Henry Hathaway to coach the All-Stars.

6. Luau gained two pounds, and judging by how he still turns up his nose at the low-cal cat food, the lizard population around our house must be in deep trouble.

7. Who stole Uncle Sam remains a mystery.

As far as the police investigation went, none of the Saucersburg Park neighbors remembered seeing a Porta Potty in motion on Memorial Day. And that "one more avenue left to explore" Mom had mentioned in the car? It turned out that was the contents of all the park trash cans from Memorial Day. Officer Krichels had forgotten to confiscate Sam Banner's clothes, and he had forgotten to search the Porta Potty for clues, but he remembered one thing: He had the patrol officers pick up the trash in case clues happened to be stashed inside. And since Memorial Day, ten trash bags had been stored in the evidence room at the police station. That was almost a month now, and it was getting pretty smelly, Mom reported. But with summer staffing problems, nobody had had time to sift through them.

Not to mention nobody really wanted to. *Yech!*

Yasmeen's family got back from the shore on a Sunday, and Monday morning I went over to the Popps' house to say welcome home. Yasmeen's parents had already left for work, and she was in the kitchen making pancakes. Jeremiah was sitting at the kitchen table, studying the sports section. I bet he did nothing but calculate baseball statistics at the shore, too. I bet his toes never even got sandy.

Yasmeen told me about her trip—lots of miniature golf like all the other years—and I caught her up on what had been happening around here, including the case we weren't going to investigate.

"*We* could look through that trash," she volunteered.

"*Gross!*" Jeremiah said.

For once I agreed with Jeremiah. "I'm pretty

sure that's a job for trained professionals," I said. "And besides, we aren't going to—"

"—investigate. I *know*, Alex. But I've got a week before engineering camp starts. Aren't you *bored*? When does All-Stars start?"

I was a little bored, but I wasn't going to admit that to Yasmeen. "The first practice is today."

"I can't believe they picked you," Jeremiah said. "Your stats aren't that good."

"Jeremiah!" Yasmeen said.

"Aw, it's okay, Yasmeen," I said. "He's right. I'm just rounding out the squad. I'll probably play the minimum, but it'll be fun anyway. I like baseball."

Yasmeen had just served my pancakes when the phone rang. Jeremiah dived for it, but Yasmeen was quicker. She said hello, listened for a few seconds, then said, "Yes, that's right. My friend Alex Parakeet and I." Pause. "Right, and his cat. But who told you about it?" And, "I see. I didn't realize that." Pause. "Sure! I have to take my little brother to his camp first." Pause. "Bring Luau? Okay, no problem." Pause. "Okay, see you then. Bye."

When Yasmeen hung up, I asked her, "Now

what?" Only it came out more like "Ow uh?" because my mouth was full.

She explained that the call was from the police reporter at *The Middle Daily Times.* "His name's Tim Roberts," she went on. "He said he's been wanting to do a follow-up on Coach Banner's kidnapping. He was looking through the old police reports, and the one about the ransom note got him interested again, so he wants to interview us."

"What was the part about Luau?" I asked.

"He wondered if we could bring Luau with us. He wants to take a picture, and he thinks Luau will make it more unusual."

"No way," I said.

"Why not? It's not like you're busy or anything."

"Because of my hair!" I said. "*Obviously.*"

Jeremiah looked up at me. "I was wondering what happened to it," he said. "Electric shock?"

"Very funny," I said. "Luau shared my pillow last night. I slept on it wrong."

"Don't worry, bud," Yasmeen said. "Hair I know how to fix."

Chapter Seventeen

Yasmeen's idea for fixing my hair was to give me a squirt of the puffy white goop her mom uses. Mousse, you call it.

"Will it really make my hair stay?" I asked. We were standing in the Popps' downstairs bathroom, staring into the mirror.

"Absolutely, bud," Yasmeen said. "My mom's hair never goes anywhere."

I flattened a couple of strands and turned my head so I could see the sides.

Yasmeen rolled her eyes. *"Come on,"* she said. "It'll be fine. I told Tim Roberts eleven o'clock, and we've still got to get Luau and take Jeremiah over to Groundhog Park for day camp."

"How do you think we're going to get Luau all the way downtown, anyway?" I asked.

"We'll walk him," Yasmeen said. "You go get his leash."

I knew walking Luau was a bad idea, and I was right. He kept sitting down to wash his face. The more I tried to explain to him that we were in a hurry, the more he swished his tail and glared at me: *The fact that you are in a hurry does not in any way alter the fact that I am not in a hurry.*

We managed to get Jeremiah to his day camp at the park, but after that I had to carry Luau. We were late, my arms were tired, and the day was getting hotter and hotter when a car horn beeped behind me. "Hey, kids! Where ya goin'? Need a ride?"

Yes! I thought, but Yasmeen said under her breath, "Oh shoot."

I turned and saw it was Mrs. Sikora, Sofie's mom, in her silver Cadillac SUV. She had stopped at the intersection and was smiling and waving out her window.

"Hi, Mrs. Sikora," Yasmeen said. "That's okay. We're fine."

"No, we're not!" I told Yasmeen. Then I turned toward Mrs. Sikora and gave her my friendliest smile. I didn't want to carry my heavy cat another step. "We'd love a ride."

"Hop in, then!"

I jumped in the backseat fast, and, with no real choice, Yasmeen climbed in next to me.

Before our seat belts were even buckled, Mrs. Sikora gunned the car through the intersection on the yellow light. "So nice to see the two of you," she said, glancing at me in the rearview mirror. "I've been reading about you, but it seems like we don't run into each other so much. Of course, Sofie saw you all year at school, but I . . ."

Mrs. Sikora talks as much as her daughter. I didn't really mean to stop listening, but after a while I couldn't help it. She was saying something about their dog, Charlie, and about their backyard, and then about how he was practically in a coma, and they had to go to the vet, which cost a fortune. I didn't want to be rude—I really was grateful for this ride—so I nodded and smiled about once every thirty seconds. After a while she said something about Sofie and her summer and friends. Or maybe how Sofie didn't have friends, which made more sense. I just kept nodding and smiling.

Luau was sitting in my lap with his head on my knees, tail in my face, looking more alert than I felt. After a few blocks he dug his claws into me. *Are you paying attention, Alex?*

We were almost to the newspaper office when I realized Mrs. Sikora had paused, and she was looking at me again in the rearview mirror, like I was supposed to say something.

"Uh . . . I'm sorry. Could you repeat that?" I stuck my fingers in my ears like maybe I hadn't heard her so well on account of wax.

"I'm just saying how grateful I am to both of you," Mrs. Sikora said. "Believe me, I love my daughter, but I know her social skills are not always up to the refined level I'd like to see. Tomorrow then? Tomorrow morning?"

By then she had pulled the SUV up to the curb outside the newspaper office. I slung Luau over my shoulder, undid my seat belt, and pulled the door handle. "Sure! Great!" I said. "Thanks again for the ride, Mrs. Sikora!"

The car had barely pulled out of the space when Yasmeen put her hands on her hips, leaned practically into my face, and laid into me. *"Why did you say that?"* she asked. *"I'll go crazy if I have to spend a day with Sofie Sikora!"*

"A day with Sofie Sikora?" I said.

"That's what you agreed to, you idiot! Weren't

you listening? Now she's got us talked into spending a whole day with her tomorrow!"

"Oops," I said.

Luau arched his back and licked a paw. *Don't say I didn't warn you.*

On our way inside I ran my fingers through my hair, which felt kind of stiff and sticky with that stuff in it.

"Hey, Yasmeen," I said, "is my hair okay?"

She looked over at me, then tightened up her lips. Was she trying not to laugh? "Yeah, sure," she said. "Come on."

The newspaper office is a two-story brick building. We pushed the swinging glass doors open and went inside. When Yasmeen explained why we were there, the receptionist barely looked up—she just pointed upstairs to the second floor. I don't think she even noticed I had a big orange cat in my arms.

I had never been in a newspaper office before. All the reporters worked together in a big, loud, busy room. Their desks had nameplates on them. Tim Roberts turned out to be a skinny guy who didn't look exactly grown-up, more like one of the students at the college. He even had pimples on his chin. He was wearing jeans and a blue button-down shirt and Adidas. He got us a couple of chairs and thanked us for coming down so quickly.

"And with the cat, too. Awesome!" he said. "Hi, kitty." He reached over and patted Luau's head—pat, pat, pat—the way someone who doesn't know much about animals does it.

"We weren't that busy," I explained to Tim Roberts, truthfully.

He laughed. "No camps? No swim lessons? No soccer? My mom always kept me busier in the summer than I was in the school year."

"I've got engineering camp starting after Fourth of July," Yasmeen said, "but this is time off. Alex has baseball."

"PYB Summer All-Stars?" Tim Roberts said. "You must be pretty good." He swiveled his chair and typed something into the computer. The monitor faced away from us so I couldn't see what. "I've been hearing all that gossip about professionalizing it, too. Is there a pro contract in your future?"

"I hope so," I said.

"Now correct me if I'm wrong," he went on, "but Sam Banner, the kidnap victim—he was your baseball coach, right, Alex?"

"He's the All-Star coach, too," I said.

"Is that why the two of you got the ransom letter, do you think?" he asked.

"It was more because of our reputation, because people know we solved those other two cases," Yasmeen said.

"I saw the magazine article," Tim Roberts said. "That was some picture of you, dude," he said. I felt my face go red. "But hey," he went on, "except for the hair, you're not half so funny-looking in person as I expected you to be."

"What's the matter with my hair?" I asked, but Tim Roberts had swiveled back to his computer and he asked another question instead of answering.

"So, kids, how's the investigation going?" He looked up at us expectantly.

"Uhhhh . . . ," Yasmeen said, "we're not investigating anything, uh . . . at the present time."

"Not investigating! How can that be?" he asked. "The police have all but given up. You're not doing anything else—you just said so. So why not? The way I look at it—you've got a responsibility here!" He shook his head. "That must've been one confused kidnapper to send a letter *after* the victim had already been freed."

"Actually," Yasmeen said, "the kidnapper sent it *before* Mr. Banner returned safely. He sent it even before the kidnapping happened. See, it came in the mail the day after Memorial Day, which was Monday, and there was no mail on Sunday—so it had to have been mailed on Saturday."

Tim Roberts typed some more and said, "Aha! Very interesting. I hadn't put that together for myself yet. So it seems to me, whether you admit it or not, that you *are* investigating."

Tim Roberts's statement hung in the air while Yasmeen and I looked at each other. One thing about living next door to each other since we were babies, sometimes we kind of read each other's mind. At that moment Yasmeen was thinking, He's right.

And I was thinking, I know I'm gonna be sorry about this, but okay—just one last time. Because it turns out *not* investigating takes almost as much brainpower as actually investigating. I can't help it— I think about the case all the time because I really do want to know who kidnapped Coach Banner.

Yasmeen turned to Tim Roberts and announced the kid sleuths were back in business.

"Good for you!" he said. "Now let me just be sure I've got the basic information, right, okay?"

And he asked us about the spellings of our names, our addresses, and our parents' names. Then he said, "Let's take some pictures."

I put my hands on my head to see what my hair was up to. It felt like a relief map of skyscrapers. "Do we have to?" I asked.

"Maybe you want to take a look in the restroom mirror first?" Tim Roberts said.

The restroom mirror was the last thing I wanted. I was afraid of what I might see. "Let's get it over with," I said.

Tim Roberts grabbed a camera from a metal cabinet by the wall. Then he led me and Yasmeen and Luau to a room the newspaper staff uses for pictures.

I stood in front of a white screen with a very unhappy Luau squirming in my arms. Yasmeen stood next to us. "A little closer, closer . . ." Tim Roberts said. "Okay, smile!" As soon as the camera started clicking, Luau forgot his annoyance, raised his head all lionlike, and posed. *This is my good side. No, wait—maybe this is my good side. Aw, heck. They're* both *my good side.*

Tim Roberts clicked away on the shutter for what seemed like a century. Then he looked down at the choices on the back of the camera

and smiled. "Want to see?" He held the camera out.

"No," I growled.

Yasmeen took a look. "I think they're all fine.
Take your pick. But are you *sure* you don't want to
see?" she asked me.

"I'm sure," I said.

Luau's tail whipped back and forth. *How come
no one ever asks me?*

We followed Tim Roberts back into the main
newsroom. Yasmeen reached over and took Luau
from me. Holding him like a baby, she looked
down into his face and said, "You look good in *all*
the pictures, kitty. Don't worry."

"Hey, wait," I said, suspiciously. "Yasmeen, did
you understand what Luau was saying just then?"

A funny expression crossed Yasmeen's face.
"Understand what Luau was saying with his tail?
I . . ." She looked down at Luau again. "It was just
obvious, bud. I mean, not like your famous telepathic cat conversations or anything."

Tim Roberts shook our hands and thanked
us for coming in. As we were leaving he said, "And
don't worry, Alex. I don't think they'll run the picture very big, and it will probably be on an inside
page. I bet nobody you know even sees it."

Chapter Eighteen

Yasmeen and I took turns carrying Luau on the way home. It was a long hot walk, and we didn't talk much because all three of us were crabby. By the time we got back to Chickadee Court, I had to change for baseball practice. Even so, Yasmeen wanted to get started on the investigation, so she invited me to eat dinner at her house that night.

The first All-Star practice was at Saucersburg Park. Dad drove me. Josh was the only other guy from Lawn Care. Ordinarily a kid who played as little as he did during the regular season would never be on the team, but that home run had convinced everyone he was a potential star. Also it was kind of traditional for the All-Star coach's kid to get to play. I only hoped Josh and his dad had declared a truce.

Besides Josh and me, eleven other guys had made the All-Star team. I knew most of them a little bit, either from school or summer camps. A couple—Denton and Sergio—went to Yasmeen's church, and Ari goes to my school and lives around the corner from me. It didn't take long for me to figure out how much better everybody was than the Lawn Care guys. Here's one way I could measure: I only chased one overthrown ball into the parking lot all afternoon. That one happened to roll under Coach Hathaway's old truck, and I noticed that the pile of books on the seat was bigger than ever. On top was that one I'd had in my lap that day he drove me to practice, *The Monkey Wrench Gang* by Edward Abbey. While I jogged back to the field, I wondered again about the title. Was it about monkeys?

After practice the coaches called a short meeting of kids and parents in the bleachers. There were two announcements: First, Coach Banner and his wife invited all of us and our families to a cookout at their house on Monday, July 3. It was supposed to be a getting-to-know-each-other event because we'd all be spending a lot of time together this summer. Second, Coach Banner announced that the commissioners had scheduled an exhibition game against the Marion Run All-Stars for the Fourth of July. "Exhibition" meant it didn't count for anything. It was really just a fancy scrimmage, but since it was a holiday, parents were invited, too.

"And afterward, there will be the traditional fireworks in Saucersburg Park," Coach Banner said.

"I thought they all burned up," Ari said.

"They did, but the patriotic spirit of the Saucersburg volunteer firefighters prevailed," said Coach Banner. "They have rallied to raise money for a new supply, and the show will go on!"

Something about the way Coach Hathaway and Coach Banner were acting—real smiley and friendly—made me think of my parents after a fight, except my baseball coaches weren't holding hands. I bet they must have promised each other—and probably the commissioners, too—that they would get along no matter what.

Yasmeen's family is a lot more formal about stuff than mine is. So dinner at her house means we all sit down at the same time and say grace and use cloth napkins. Yasmeen's family doesn't even put the milk carton on the table. And conversation is supposed to be "of general interest," which means no fighting allowed.

I used to be a little scared about eating at Yasmeen's, but after a while I figured out her parents are nice and they even like kids. You just have to follow their rules.

That night we ate rice, green beans, and pot roast. I love green beans, especially with little pieces of bacon. After we said grace I did nothing but eat green beans till they were gone. I was swallowing the last bite when I realized Jeremiah was staring at me.

"You must like green beans," he said, frowning.

Mrs. Popp smiled. "It's gratifying to feed a child like Alex who's so enthusiastic about vegetables."

Jeremiah shook his head. "My teacher says you shouldn't eat so fast. My teacher says if you do, you'll get fat."

"Alex isn't fat," Yasmeen said. I was going to say thank you, but then she added, "He's just healthy."

"What's that supposed to mean?" I asked.

"Let's change the subject, shall we?" Mrs. Popp said.

"Jeremiah, didn't your day camp go to the

library for story hour this afternoon? What book did the librarian read?"

"*Curious George!*" Jeremiah said, with what counts for Jeremiah as a smile. "He's a monkey. He has a TV show. Have you ever heard of him?" He looked at his parents.

"Some commentators see Curious George as a cultural vestige of colonialism," Professor Popp said.

"No, he's a monkey," Jeremiah said. "And his friend is the man in the yellow hat."

Monkey made me think of *The Monkey Wrench Gang.* A book seemed like a safe topic "of general interest," so I asked Mrs. Popp if she had heard of it. I figured, being a librarian, she probably knew every book ever written. And I was right.

"Edward Abbey is the author," she said. "In fact, he was born not far from here—in Indiana County. I'm sure we have it in the college library if you want to borrow it. What brings it to mind, Alex?"

I explained. "I just thought the title was cool," I said. "What's it about?"

Professor Popp answered. "Ecoterrorism."

There was a clatter as Yasmeen and I both dropped our forks.

Professor Popp looked from her to me. "Why the startled reaction?"

"Remember the ransom letter from the kidnapper?" Yasmeen asked.

"Coach Banner's kidnapper," I clarified.

"Oh yes," Professor Popp nodded. "I see now. That was putatively an act of ecoterrorism as well."

"What happens in the book?" Yasmeen wanted to know. "Why 'monkey wrench'?"

"You've heard of putting a wrench in the works?" Professor Popp said.

"Like break something?" I said.

"More or less," said Professor Popp. "The idea in the book—as I remember—is that a band of young people hatch a plot to blow up a dam."

"What happened?" Yasmeen asked. "Did they do it?"

"I never read it," Professor Popp said. "It was just one of those books everyone talked about at the time—part of the radical zeitgeist."

Sometimes eating dinner at the Popps is like a really long vocabulary lesson.

"Radical zit *what*?" Jeremiah asked.

As usual, Yasmeen couldn't resist the urge to show off. "*Zeitgeist* means 'a popular idea,'"

Yasmeen said. "So I guess when the book was written, it was popular to think that radical change would be good."

"Very nice, Ms. Popp," her dad said, as if she were one of his students.

"I don't get it exactly," I said. "I mean, blowing up a dam is radical, all right. But it seems like a waste. Why would anybody want to do it?"

Professor Popp explained that a dam turns a river into a lake. Whether a dam is bad or not depends on what you want—still lake or flowing river.

"There are advantages to both," he said. "But environmentalists tend to want to keep things natural, and there are still environmentalists—apparently like your correspondent, the kidnapper—who believe any means are acceptable toward that end."

"I don't think violence is *ever* acceptable," Yasmeen said.

"Never?" Professor Popp asked. "What about if soldiers invade your country—the way the Germans invaded Poland in 1939?"

"Well," Yasmeen said thoughtfully, "I guess it's okay to fight back. Because then it's self-defense."

"Or to overthrow a bad leader—a leader who oppresses his people?" Professor Popp asked. "What about King George and the American Revolution?"

"The Boston Tea Party!" I said.

Yasmeen's mom winked at me. "Very good, Mr. Parakeet."

Yasmeen shook her head. "I guess it's not as simple as I thought."

"There are ways to protest that aren't violent," I said. "Like the marches during the Vietnam War."

"True," Mrs. Popp said. "Not to mention sit-ins during the civil rights movement. Without nonviolent protests, it would have taken a lot longer to change the laws."

"Coach Hathaway got arrested at a sit-in," I put in.

Professor Popp sniffed. "I understand Professor Hathaway was quite the firebrand in his day," he said. "And perhaps still is. That long hair. That earring." He shook his head. "Not my cup of tea."

"No, Derek," Mrs. Popp said. "But it does take all kinds, you know."

I was between bites of pot roast, and I glanced over at Yasmeen. Her eyebrows had the ferocious look they get when she's thinking. If you're Yasmeen, you don't just chew on a problem, you attack it and kill it.

It was Jeremiah's turn to help with dishes, so after we cleared the table, Yasmeen and I were free to go into the den and talk about the investigation. The Popps' den has about a million books, wood panel walls, a big old desk, and a small leather sofa. There's no TV. Yasmeen sat down in the leather desk chair and got a stack of file cards out of the drawer. She didn't say a word. She started writing.

"Hey!" I said. "We have to *talk* first. That's the way we always do it—ever since we started investigating."

Yasmeen looked up at me and said, "Oh, sorry. It's just that this time I think we can take a short-cut—skip the talking part."

"We can?" I asked. "Why?"

"Isn't it obvious?" she asked. "Because this time we already know who did it."

Chapter Nineteen

Yasmeen might have known who did it, but I didn't—and I couldn't admit that, so I stood up and started walking casually toward the desk. "Well, yeah. But we still have to follow *procedure*," I said.

"Why?" Yasmeen asked.

Why was a good question to which I did not have a good answer. But I could see the little white card. I could almost make out the words she had written on it. Another step, and—

Jeremiah came into the den. Yasmeen slipped the card under her rear end to hide it. *Shoot!*

"What are you sitting on?" Jeremiah asked her.

"Mind your own bee's wax," she said.

I saw my chance. "We might as well tell him, Yasmeen. He'll find out sooner or later anyway."

"Oh, all right." She pulled the card out and handed it to him.

Jeremiah squinted and read out loud, "Coach Henry Hathaway."

"*Coach Hathaway?*" I repeated. "Just because he's got a book in his truck?"

So much for acting like I already knew.

"Would somebody please tell me what's . . . ?" Jeremiah said, but Yasmeen and I paid no attention.

"Look at the evidence, Alex," Yasmeen said. She raised a finger for each point. "First, he's an ecoterrorist. Second, he hates Coach Banner. Third . . ." She paused. "Well, I don't entirely have a third. But first and second are enough."

"You don't even know Coach Hathaway!" I said. "If you knew him . . ." Then I stopped. *Shoot.* Yasmeen didn't have a third, but in that second I realized I did. Coach Hathaway had been a demolitions expert in Vietnam. What did that mean? Bombs. He had exactly the special knowledge needed to set off the fire, probably to release the poison gas, too.

I didn't know whether to tell her or not. I was totally sure Coach Hathaway didn't do it. But Yasmeen is my partner.

I sighed a big sigh. "There's one other thing," I said. And I explained.

"*Ha!*" she said, exactly like I was afraid she would. "Proof!"

"It is not proof!" I said. "You don't know he's an ecoterrorist. All you know is he's got a book about guys blowing up a dam."

"Why else would he be interested in stuff like that if he wasn't an ecoterrorist himself?" Yasmeen asked. "Plus he was arrested. He has criminal experience!"

"He was arrested for a *sit-in*," I said.

"A sit-in is a protest. The kidnapping was supposed to be a protest, too. Admit it—you're prejudiced because you like him."

"And *you're* prejudiced because you agree with your dad," I said. "You hate long hair."

"I hate his itsy-bitsy gold earring," Jeremiah said. "It looks like a *girl* thing."

Yasmeen turned on her brother: "And what's wrong with girl things? If I wear blue jeans is that a *boy* thing?"

Jeremiah looked at his shoelaces. "Oops," he said.

Having defeated Jeremiah, Yasmeen turned to

me. "Look, Alex," she said, "we do agree on this, anyway. We don't have enough evidence yet."

"That's for sure," I said, "because we don't have *any* evidence."

"So then we agree on something else," Yasmeen said. "The next thing we have to do is get some."

Chapter Twenty

Where's the best place to go when you want evidence?

An evidence room.

And here in College Springs that means the basement of the College Springs Police Department, where ten bags of trash collected from Saucersburg Park have been sitting in a corner for about a month. In those garbage bags is where Yasmeen thought we might find evidence against Coach Hathaway.

I had tried to talk Yasmeen out of this bright idea, but if you ask me arguing with Yasmeen is a waste of energy. The more you argue, the more she won't budge.

So I agreed to ask my mom if we could help

the police by going through the trash. We couldn't ask her that same night because she had gone to bed early. The next morning, the doorbell woke me and Luau at nine-thirty.

Luau mrrfed when I shifted him off my feet. *Leave me alone. Low-cal cat food is not worth waking up for.*

The doorbell rang again. Dad must have gone shopping.

I didn't really run down the stairs. More like I let gravity take hold and tripped down them. When I opened the front door, the bright sun made my eyes tear.

Yasmeen was standing on our front step with her bicycle. "Come on, bud. Get a move on!" she said. "We're going downtown. Remember?"

"Huh? What? We are . . . ? Okay." I yawned and obediently walked out onto the step.

Yasmeen looked at me funny. "Uh, bud?" she asked. "Are you planning to go downtown in your Bart Simpson jammies? I mean, *I* think they're cute, but . . ."

I guess total embarrassment wakes a person up because I was back in my room, dressed, and down the stairs again in about a minute. When I went into the kitchen to leave my dad a note, I found one on the table for me.

Grocery shopping, then bank, library, etc.
That's quite a do in the pho! Eat b'fast!
   D.

B'fast meant "breakfast." But *quite a do? Pho?* What was he talking about? "Hurry up!" Yasmeen yelled.

I poured Luau a bowl of his healthy, low-cal cat food, then I scribbled a note for my dad:

No time for b'fast. Going to see Mom. What's pho?
   A.

I met Yasmeen in front with my bike, and we rode the two miles downtown to where the police department is. By the time we got there, I was awake but hungry.

My mom's office is always neat and tidy. Usually there's nothing on her desk except her computer and what she's working on right at that moment. Everything else is put away. Today there was a stack of fat books and a newspaper. One of the books was open, and I read the title page upside down, *Environmental Protection Agency Guide to Estuarial Ecology, Vol. I.*

Huh?

What was she reading *that* for?

But before I could ask her, she stood up and said, "It's my celebrity guests! Have a seat. Now what can I, a mere police detective, do for two such famous sleuths as yourselves?"

Yasmeen and I looked at each other.

"Sorry, what?" I asked Mom.

"Oh, you haven't seen this?" She took the newspaper and displayed it for us. Now my dad's mysterious "pho" note made sense. On the front page of *The Middle Daily Times* was the photo Tim Roberts had taken yesterday. It was *huge*, which it had to be to accommodate all my hair, rising off my face like quills on a scared porcupine.

Yasmeen made a baby-elephant snort sound, then covered her mouth with her hands and coughed. "Well, bud," she said finally, her mouth still covered, "at least your teeth don't look so big in this one."

"He said it would be in the back! He said nobody would see it!" I could picture the grief I was gonna get from the baseball team at practice tonight, not to mention from Ashley and Teresa the next time I saw them. It was going to be worse than last time!

Mom's expression looked a little amused and a little exasperated. "Must not have been a lot of real news to report on," she said. "According to the story . . ." She put her glasses on, spread the paper out, and read: "'Famous kid sleuths Alex Parakeet and Yasmeen Popp received a ransom note from the kidnapper late last month. Since local police have effectively abandoned investigation of the mysterious kidnapping, it will be up to the youthful duo to identify the perpetrator and see that justice is done.'"

"Oh, dear," Yasmeen said, but she was grinning. Were Ashley and Teresa right? Was it true she was getting stuck-up?

"Shoot," I said. "Mom—we didn't mean—"

Mom waved her hand. "Never mind," she said, but I could tell she *did* mind. "The only thing the story doesn't say is—*How* do you plan to solve the case?"

"Well," Yasmeen said, "actually, Mrs. Parakeet, that's why we're here." Yasmeen went on and explained: We knew the police hadn't had time to examine the garbage yet, and we were willing to do it. She didn't mention the Coach Hathaway part, just said we were looking for clues.

"No way," Mom said.

"Okay, fine." I bounced out of my chair. "I mean, that's too bad, but come on, Yasmeen. I guess somebody else gets to go through the ten bags of disgusting, smelly, month-old trash. And I was looking forward to it, too. Hey, Mom? Are there any doughnuts in the break room today?"

I was ready to head for the break room, but Yasmeen didn't move. About five seconds went by, and then as I watched, my mom's face changed. It's like a switch went off in her brain, a switch that was connected to her eyebrows: They shot up; they dropped down.

"Disgusting . . . smelly . . . garbage," Mom repeated slowly. "On the other hand it might not be *such* a terrible idea. I think I told you once, Alex, that police work is often distasteful? It's not *all* about glory and recognition and the front page? Give me just one second." She stood up. "I need to talk to the chief."

The chief's office is a few doors down the hall from my mom's. She wasn't gone long, and when she came back, she was smiling. "He went for it!"

she said. "He admits it's unorthodox, but we let the Explorer Scouts do jobs like this for us sometimes. And anyway, nobody else will have a chance to go through that garbage for who knows how long."

Mom said she'd show us the evidence room and run us through appropriate procedure in a minute, but first she had to call Dad to remind him Luau had a vet appointment. He was due for a weigh-in and a general checkup at two.

She picked up the phone, then turned to me. "The cat carrier's in the basement, isn't it?" she asked.

"I think so," I said. "But he does okay in the car without it. Yesterday when Mrs. Sikora gave us a ride . . ." And that's when I remembered. *"Oh, shoot!"*

"What?" Mom asked.

Yasmeen and I looked at each other. *"Sofie!"* we said at the same time—only I said it sounding guilty, and she said it sounding annoyed.

"What about her?" Mom asked, and I explained how I'd unintentionally told Sofie's mom that Yasmeen and I would spend the day with her.

"I gotta call her," I said.

"Yeah—maybe she wants to come and sort garbage with us," Yasmeen said sarcastically.

I figured a kid as spoiled as Sofie would never say yes to sorting garbage.

Only—shows what I know—when I asked her, she agreed right away: "You mean investigate like when we solved the Halloween case together? Cool! I'll be right there!"

The PD's evidence room is a very tidy place with white-painted cinder block walls and bluish fluorescent lighting. There is a long metal table in the middle of the room that kind of reminds me of an operating table. That's where the technicians work when they're using microscopes or chemicals to process evidence. And it's where Yasmeen, Sofie, and I were going to work, too.

Sergeant Ahn was in the evidence room as well. He was in charge of us, but he was sitting on a stool at a counter on the other side of the room wearing a headset so he could listen to taped evidence in another case. We could work on our own, provided we told him if we needed to leave or if we found anything important.

The first trash bag was labeled SOUTHEAST COR-NER, SAUCERSBURG PARK, ADJACENT TO PENFIELD ALLEY.

"Ready?" Yasmeen asked.

"Yes sirree," Sofie said, like the black plastic bag was full of Christmas presents. Did the girl not have a functioning nose or what?

I scrunched up my own nostrils and nodded. Yasmeen undid the twisty tie. The smell—green mold meets cat poop laced with rotting fruit— made my stomach jump into my throat and my eyes start to water. Even Sergeant Ahn across the room put a hand on his belly and said, *"Ewww,"* and he's a professional law enforcement officer who has seen and smelled some pretty disgusting stuff.

"I don't think I can do this," I said, exhaling through my nose.

"Oh, stop bein' a weenie," said Sofie Sikora. "What's a little smelliness compared to solving a crime? What's our first item, Yasmeen? Give it over, and I'll take its picture."

Mom had handed us each a pair of plastic gloves like doctors wear; then she said something half joking like, "I hereby deputize you in the name of the citizens of College Springs." After that she explained what we were supposed to do. The idea was that Yasmeen would remove each piece of trash from the bag and say what it was, I would write this down on a special piece of paper coded and indexed for evidence, and Sofie would take a picture with the department's digital camera. Then we put the item in a box labeled EVIDENCE. Part of what I had to write down was an identifier number so the item could be matched with the photo and the box later.

"Candy wrapper, Snickers," Yasmeen said.

I wrote this on a line on the form.

Click. Sofie took the picture. Yasmeen pulled out a plastic cup. "Plastic cup," she said. "Lipstick stains." I wrote this down, lipstick included. *Click*. Sofie put the plastic cup next to the Snickers wrapper in the box.

Already I could see this was going to take a long time.

The fourth item was a water bottle. So was the fifth item. Then came a slippery black something covered with white and green and yellow spots that had once been—I hope—a banana peel. I thought it was pretty much as disgusting as a thing could get till Yasmeen pulled out the next item, a diaper.

Even Sofie made a sick face.

As far as the police were concerned, we were logging evidence in. As far as Yasmeen and

I were concerned, though, we were looking for clues—meaning anything unusual. It took us about fifteen minutes to go through a trash bag; and after four were done, we had figured out that the most usual things were partially eaten food, cigarette butts, plastic utensils, fast-food bags, wadded-up paper, and soda bottles, water bottles, juice bottles—lots of bottles. The one-of-a-kind things we found were a ripped gray T-shirt, size XL; a dirty white sock; a broken necklace made out of pink plastic beads; and a used-up tube of ChapStick.

None of them exactly told us who the kidnapper was—or proved that the kidnapper *wasn't* Coach Hathaway.

After the third trash bag, I realized the smell wasn't bothering me as much. And after the seventh one, I remembered I was hungry. I hadn't eaten breakfast, remember—hadn't even gotten my chocolate doughnut from the break room. It sounds sick that I could be looking at old garbage and thinking about chocolate doughnuts, but the stomach is a strange and wonderful thing.

We were on the bag labeled NORTHWEST CORNER BY THE DRINKING FOUNTAIN, when I asked if we could stop for lunch.

"We're almost done," Yasmeen said. "Let's just finish the last two."

"Who put you in charge?" Sofie asked her.

Yasmeen ignored Sofie. "McDonald's french fries wrapper," she said. "Greasy."

I wrote it down. But instead of taking the picture, Sofie said, "You shouldn't let her boss you around, Alex."

"I'm not letting her," I said. "She's right. We can finish up, then have lunch. That's okay with me. Take the picture."

Sofie frowned then—*click*—she took the picture.

I finished writing "greasy" and waited for Yasmeen to identify the next item; but she didn't say anything, and after a few seconds, I looked up to see why. Yasmeen was holding something made out of brown plastic. It was a little smaller than a deck of cards and had a big white button in the middle. She turned it over and smiled and turned it over again. I didn't recognize the plastic thing at first—ours looks different—and I couldn't figure out why Yasmeen would be smiling.

But then Sofie Sikora said, "Garage-door opener. So what?"

And Yasmeen looked at me and said, "Alex, bud, I think this case will soon be closed."

Chapter Twenty-one

Yasmeen likes to say I am not as dumb as I look, and she's right. I mean, as soon as I realized the brown plastic thing was a garage-door opener, I realized what it might mean to the case: A remote control probably released the gas that put Coach Banner to sleep in the Porta Potty. A remote control probably set off the fire in the fireworks shed.

A garage-door opener is a remote control.

Sofie didn't know about the gas, and she didn't know that the fire was arson, but it was obvious from the way Yasmeen was acting that there was something very important about this latest find from the trash bag.

"Whose garage does that open, anyway?" Sofie

asked. "I bet you think you know, don't you? I bet you think it's the kidnapper's!"

Sofie was taking wild guesses, but they were extremely good wild guesses. And Yasmeen is not much of an actress. "How did you know?" Yasmeen asked. "I mean . . . I mean . . ." She tried to suck the words back, but one thing about words: When they get out of your mouth, they're gone forever.

"Where does he live—the kidnapper?" Sofie was off and running. "Can we go there? Can we test the opener out?"

"Sofie!" I protested. "This might be evidence in a criminal case! We can't steal it!"

Sofie gave me a shocked and hurt look. "I would *never* say steal it!" She shook her head solemnly. "That would be wrong. I'm just saying 'borrow' it for a few minutes. We finish this up; then we go. We can get doughnuts on the way. I've got money in my pocket. I never travel without money in my pocket. I've usually got quite a lot of money, actually—and I know your family's poor, Alex, so I can buy you a doughnut, provided you pay me back—maybe when your dad gets a job again. After we catch the kidnapper, we'll bring the door opener right back and tell the police what we know; and then we'll go to the newspaper and be heroes. Gosh"—she yanked a few strands of her blond hair—"I hope my hair looks okay for the pictures. Your hair looked awful in the picture in the newspaper today, Alex, like that movie about Frankenstein's wife, what's-it-called? Does he live far away—the kidnapper, I mean? Not Frankenstein. Who is it, Yazzie? Alex? *Who is it?*"

You could tell how desperate Sofie was to know because she actually paused and waited for an answer—didn't just keep talking the way she usually does.

"Sofie, that clicker deal there," I said slowly, thinking while I talked, "it might not have anything to do with the case at all. . . . Besides, I have no idea where Coach Hathaway lives. If it's out in Belletoona or something, it's too far to bike."

"*Coach Hathaway?*" Sofie said.

"*Alex!*" Yasmeen said.

"Oops," I said.

"Coach Hathaway's the kidnapper? Cool!"

Sofie was so excited she clapped her hands and Sergeant Ahn looked over.

"Everything all right, kids?" he asked, shutting off the machine he had been listening to. "Found anything good?"

We all shook our heads and answered at pretty much the same time: "Uh-uh," "No," "Nothing."

Sergeant Ahn nodded like he didn't notice anything strange. "Tedious work, isn't it. Let me know if you need help."

"We will," "Okay," "For sure."

Sergeant Ahn pushed the button and went back to listening.

After that Sofie tried to speak more softly. "I never did trust Coach Hathaway—I don't like old guys with ponytails. Let's look him up in the phone book!"

"How do you even know Coach Hathaway?" I asked her.

"He coached Byron's team one year," she said. "I don't know where he lives, but I don't think it's Belletoona."

"I know where he lives," Yasmeen said. "We could be there in like ten minutes."

Now it was my turn to be exasperated. "*Yasmeen!*"

"But it's not like we're going to go," she said quickly. "We're going to just put this opener in the box like everything else, only we'll tell Alex's mom about it. It's up to the police to—"

"—to sit on it for another month without doing anything!" Sofie said.

"*Shhh!*" Yasmeen and I said at the same time.

Sofie glanced over at Sergeant Ahn, then said in a whisper: "Everybody's on vacation or busy—that's what Tim Roberts's story in the paper today said. They don't care who stole Uncle Sam! But I *totally* care! Plus I want to have my picture in the paper. And my mom says if I solve a crime, it'll look good on my college application."

"No," Yasmeen said.

"So you're like the boss now, boss lady?" Sofie said. "What do you say, Alex?"

I tried to put my eyes anywhere but on Yasmeen and Sofie. They were both looking at me.

"It's up to *you* to decide," Yasmeen said. "I say we can't 'borrow' the door opener to test it out, and Sofie says we've got to—a one-to-one vote. In a democracy majority rules, and the United States is a democracy. So it's up to you."

I spoke slowly to buy time. "Before we go any-place," I said, "we've got to log in the opener as evidence and finish up the last trash bag. Yasmeen's right."

"*But how do we decide what to do?*" Sofie wasn't being quiet anymore.

"Uh . . . Rock, Paper, Scissors?" I suggested.

Yasmeen loves Rock, Paper, Scissors. "Good idea!" she said. "What do you say, Sofie?"

"Deal."

Yasmeen rolled her shoulders and shook out her fingers. Sofie spit (*yech!*) on her palms and rubbed them together. Glaring at each other they pumped their fists:

"*Rock, Paper, Scissors*—shoot!"

Chapter Twenty-two

Fifteen minutes after we left the police station, Yasmeen, Sofie, and I were standing on the sidewalk in front of three small stone houses on Lime Tree Lane, which is between downtown and the college campus.

"Come on, Yazzie, which one is it?" Sofie asked.

"Would you stop calling me Yazzie!" Yasmeen snapped.

"You're just mad because I beat you at Rock, Paper, Scissors," Sofie said. "And now it turns out you don't even know which house he lives in."

"I do, too," Yasmeen said. "I was in it once because he and my mom were working on some study together. It's right here." She pointed at the house in front of us. "Or else there." She pointed at the one next door. "Or . . . possibly there." She pointed down the street.

We had logged in the opener as evidence—taken its picture and everything—and finished up the last trash bag. After that we gave Sergeant Ahn the trash and all the paperwork. Then he walked us down the hall and out of the basement exit, while all the time Sofie had the opener in her pocket. I had pretty much convinced myself that "borrowing" evidence was okay because the police were too busy to work on this investigation themselves. But now standing on the sidewalk, I started to feel guilty.

"What if Coach Hathaway's home?" I asked. "What if he comes out and sees us? How do we explain what we're doing here?"

"We'll say we've got a summer job," Sofie said, like she had it all worked out.

"A summer job doing what?" I asked.

"Taking surveys," Sofie said, "for a candy company."

Yasmeen paused in front of the second house, and we stopped, too.

"Where did you come up with an idea like that?" I asked Sofie.

She shrugged. "We should think of some question we're asking. Like, the candy company would want to know what people want to eat. So maybe a good question is: Tell me, sir, on a scale of one to ten, what kind of candy do you like best?"

Yasmeen looked back at us. "That's a stupid question," she said. "It doesn't even make sense." We started walking toward the third house, but halfway there Sofie stopped in the middle of the sidewalk.

"Hey!" she said. "You guys! It doesn't matter which house it is!" She pulled the opener out of her pocket and looked at each of us. "I'll just aim this at the garages, and the one that opens has to be Coach Hathaway's—right?"

Yasmeen and I locked eyes. Why didn't we think of that?

We walked a few more steps till we were standing in front of the third house, then we turned to face it. Sofie held up the opener. "Ready." She pointed it at the innocent-looking garage. "Aim." She pressed the button. "*Fire!*"

I was half expecting the garage to vaporize, or go up in flames, or at least glow a little—but what really happened was—nothing.

I didn't want my baseball coach to be a kidnapper, but this was still a little disappointing. Sofie didn't seem to mind, though.

"Okay, it's not this one," she said. "Come on."

We headed back down the sidewalk. As we walked toward the next stone house, I thought about how we had been lucky. We hadn't seen anybody at all—not even a kid on a tricycle. And nobody had asked what we were doing here, either. But about one second after I finished that thought, a College Springs police cruiser turned the corner and came slowly down the block.

My heart jumped. *"Hide!"* I looked around for convenient, empty, kid-sized boxes while Yasmeen looked at the sky in case an angel might save us.

Sofie shook her head and shot us disgusted looks. "What a couple of lame babies," she said. "How did you ever get along before I showed up?" She turned and waved at the cruiser, then glanced over her shoulder at us, and commanded, *"Smile."*

The cruiser coasted up beside us. The driver rolled down the window. It was Officer Krichels.

Sofie spoke before he had a chance to. "Hi, Officer Krichels! What's the haps?" Yasmeen and I smiled. I might have overdone it. My cheeks hurt.

Officer Krichels nodded but didn't return our smiles. "Afternoon, kids. Nice picture in the paper this morning. Love the hair, Alex. Have you signed on with the supersleuths, too, Sofie?"

"Me? Ha-ha—not me! We're just over here because . . ." She looked at me and hesitated. She must've remembered Yasmeen and I hadn't been so keen on her earlier idea.

"Because we got summer jobs," I said, "doing a survey for a candy company."

"Did you now?" Officer Krichels said skeptically. "And what sort of survey would that be?"

"Oh, you know," Yasmeen said. "We ask questions like, On a scale of one to ten, what kind of candy do you like best?"

Officer Krichels took that in and nodded slowly. "Hershey bar, no almonds," he said. "It's a ten, and it's made right here in Pennsylvania."

"We'll be sure and report that to our employer," Sofie said, "whose identity we are not at liberty to disclose."

Officer Krichels nodded again. "Of course not," he said. "Well, if you'll excuse me, I got my own job to do. It's not glamorous. We don't get our picture in the papers much. Nobody even gives us free candy bars. Nevertheless, there are still a few folks who think that catching criminals and keeping the public safe is important."

"We know that, Officer Krichels," I started to say. "My mom . . ." But already the window was back up, and the car was moving away from us.

I looked at Yasmeen. "Everyone's mad at us," I said. "But we didn't ask to have our pictures in a magazine or the newspaper!"

"And they think I'm stuck-up," Yasmeen said sadly.

"What are you guys apologizing for?" Sofie said. "It's *good* to solve crimes! It's *good* to be famous! I only wish I was, too."

By now we had walked down to the next driveway. "Here, Yasmeen," Sofie handed her the clicker. "Your turn."

Yasmeen smiled, surprised. "Thanks."

Yasmeen aimed carefully, like this was target practice, then she closed her eyes and clicked. I didn't expect anything to happen. There were a thousand reasons that garage wasn't going to open, including the obvious one, that Coach Hathaway wasn't the kidnapper. That's why, when I heard the first squeak, I didn't connect it to the door at all. I thought it must be a bird or car brakes or something, and I started looking around. But I didn't see anything squeaky, and I looked back up the driveway—and that's when I realized it was the springs of the garage door. Their whining was soon followed by a groan that made Sofie, Yasmeen, and me all gasp at once, and then . . . slowly . . . the door began to open.

Chapter Twenty-three

The garage door rose. Our jaws dropped. We all took a couple of steps back, like we expected a tiger to charge us.

"It might be a coincidence," I said, and I noticed my voice was squeaky like the door.

"It is not a coincidence," Yasmeen said.

"Come on," Sofie said once the door was open. She began walking up the driveway.

"*Wait a minute!*" Yasmeen called after her. "Going in was never part of the deal. We just wanted to see if this was *his* clicker."

Sofie didn't look back, and I knew Yasmeen was thinking the same as me, that the last thing she wanted to do was walk into that dark garage, the garage of a *kidnapper*. But we couldn't let Sofie go alone, so we followed. As we got closer I could see the outline of all sorts of shapes in the garage, but no car.

"He's not home," I whispered.

"We can't be sure," Yasmeen whispered back. "The garage looks pretty full of junk. Probably he doesn't keep his car in here anyway."

We arrived at the line where the driveway asphalt changed to the concrete of the garage floor. I stopped and peered inside—boxes, a work-bench, tools, baseball equipment, tangled bicycles, a shovel, a lawn mower, some chairs—none of it arranged in any order. Beside me Sofie hesitated; I was hoping maybe she would get some sense and retreat, but instead she yelled, "*Anybody home?*"

"*Shhh!*" Yasmeen and I hissed.

"Oh, come on. What's he gonna do"—Sofie asked—"lock us up in a Porta Potty? Let's look around. Maybe we'll find another clue—some detonators or fuses or nitro or something."

"I wouldn't do that." Coach Hathaway's voice is deep, and now the garage echoed with it. Even Sofie jumped. "It's not safe," the voice added, and then a light went on.

Coach Hathaway was standing in a far corner by a door that must've led out to the backyard.

Even though it was a warm day, he was wearing a navy blue hoodie and athletic shorts. Had he been in that corner all along? Had he watched us walk up the driveway? Was this whole thing a trap?

"What are you doing in my garage?" Coach Hathaway asked. "And where did you find my opener? I've been looking all over for it."

One thing I've learned in the detective business: When you find out somebody is the bad guy, they all of a sudden look different to you—scary, even if before they looked nice. That's what happened with Coach Hathaway now. His eyes, which I had thought were sky blue, looked all of a sudden icy, and his narrow face with the smile wrinkles looked like a toothy rat's.

Sofie recovered first.

"We're arresting you," she said forcefully, "on charges of stealing Coach Banner!"

"*No, we're not!*" I said. "I mean, it's not like we're police or anything. Sofie doesn't know what she's talking about. She's . . . uh . . ."

" . . . delusional," Yasmeen said.

I nodded.

"It means she has delusions," Yasmeen said, helpfully.

"I do not," Sofie said. "We know you stole

179

Coach Banner; and if you'll go ahead and confess, it'll save a lot of time. My mom wants me home by three."

I shook my head in amazement. I don't care how brave Sofie is or how smart, we are *never* bringing her with us on an investigation again.

"I'm afraid confessing isn't on the to-do list," Coach Hathaway said. "Do I know you?"

"I'm Byron's sister," Sofie said. "He was on your team last year. Remember?"

"Ah yes, you're the loquacious one," Coach Hathaway said.

"*Loquacious* means—" Yasmeen started to explain, but Sofie cut her off.

"We have no choice but to place you under arrest, uh . . . in the name of the citizens of College Springs, Pennsylvania. Now if you'll just come quietly, my associates won't have to get rough with you."

Her associates? Was that Yasmeen and me?

"And just where"—Coach Hathaway unfolded his arms and took a step toward us—"are we going?" His voice was low and ominous.

Sofie mirrored Coach Hathaway's move. She took her hands out of her pockets and rolled her shoulders like she was limbering up. Now the two of them were squared off right there in the garage.

"Downtown," Sofie said.

I didn't know what Sofie planned to do, but I did know I couldn't let her do it alone. So I took a step forward to back her up, and good old Yasmeen was right with me.

A long second passed; then quick as a feline, Sofie sprang at Coach Hathaway and knocked him off balance.

"*Help me, you weenies!*" she yelled, while at the same time she was pummeling my baseball coach. "I can't capture a kidnapper all alone!"

"*Ow! Ow!*" Coach Hathaway hollered. "*Sofie—* cut it out! *Uncle!*"

Somehow in the tussle, the two of them bumped into the light switch and the garage-door button on the wall behind him so that the garage was plunged into darkness just as the door started to drop. I might have been able to limbo my way under it and out—but I was paralyzed by fear and indecision. Moments later the door closed, and we were trapped.

"No fair pulling hair! *Ow!*" I heard Coach Hathaway holler. Then there were the thumps and clatters and *oofs* that go with a struggle. Finally everything got quiet except for a whole lot of breathless panting, and then the light came on again. What it revealed was Coach Hathaway standing in a different corner of the garage. His hair had been yanked out of its usual ponytail and hung wild. He was sweaty and had a streak of grime across his face. He looked like a crazy man—even more crazy because he held a squirming, kicking girl under his arm.

"*Let me down, you bully!*" Sofie yelled.

"Don't hurt her!" I said.

"Me hurt *her?*" Coach Hathaway said. "What about the other way—"

"Put her down," Yasmeen said firmly. I looked over, and she was brandishing the garage-door opener, aiming it right at Coach Hathaway's head. "If you don't put her down, I'll . . . I'll . . ."

" . . . shoot me with my own garage-door opener?" Coach Hathaway said.

"Yes," Yasmeen said, like this made perfect sense. "But only if I have to."

Coach Hathaway looked at the door opener, at me, and then down at Sofie, who glared up at him like death and punched the air for good measure. Then he started laughing. "Look," he said at last. "You kids have kind of forced my hand here, and I think all in all it'd be a good idea if you take a look at something before I let you go. Sofie?" He looked down at her. "I'm gonna set you down, but you gotta promise, no more beating up on me, okay? At least not till you see what I've got to show you."

When Sofie grunted a grudging, "Okay," he set her down.

Without another word Coach Hathaway unzipped his hoodie. This made my heart thump again, and Sofie took a step back. Did he have a weapon more lethal than a garage-door opener? But no. When he opened the hoodie, it revealed an inside pocket, and clipped to the pocket was a big silver badge in a black leather wallet, just like on TV.

I gasped. "FBI?"

"Interpol?" Yasmeen said.

"CIA?" Sofie said.

Coach Hathaway shook his head. "Pennsylvania Youth Baseball. Special Agent K, at your service."

Chapter Twenty-four

There was an ID photo in the wallet with the badge, and Sofie, Yasmeen, and I studied it. The photo was Coach Hathaway, all right, wearing a black baseball cap with PYB in red letters. He looked serious and cool, the way a special agent was supposed to look—the way I never look.

"I didn't know Youth Baseball *had* special agents," Sofie said. Her voice was skeptical, and I guess it did sound kind of unlikely.

"It's a relatively new thing," Coach Hathaway said. "We're all volunteers, charged with protecting the integrity of the sport so that young people will be able to play without being subject to corrupting influences."

"But why is it a secret?" Yasmeen asked. "Are you undercover?"

"That's the part I didn't want to get into," Coach Hathaway said. "Kids, I'm working on a special assignment. Only a few people know about it, and I'd appreciate it if you kept this conversation of ours confidential. If you don't it could jeopardize the good name of youth baseball—and perhaps the health and safety of some friends of mine as well. One man, as you know, has already been kidnapped. Can I count on you?"

"Wait a minute," Yasmeen said. "Are you investigating the kidnapping, too?"

"Oh, that's just *great*!" Sofie put her hands on her hips and stomped her foot. "I bet after I did all this work, you get to catch the kidnapper! That means your picture will be in the paper and not mine. I bet I *never* get my picture in the paper. And it's not like *you* went through a zillion bags of smelly trash this morning! This is just so *unfair*."

"Smelly trash?" Coach Hathaway said. "Is that where you found my garage-door opener?"

"It's a long story," Yasmeen said.

"I see." Coach Hathaway nodded thoughtfully. "But I didn't say I'm investigating the kidnapping, did I?"

"Well, are you?" Sofie said.

"I'm not at liberty—"

"Oh foo on liberty!" Sofie said, and then she turned to Yasmeen and me. "I'm going home. Next time you guys have a crime to solve, call somebody else."

Sofie wheeled around and strode away from us up the driveway. But after about five strides, she slowed down; and when she got to the sidewalk, she stopped. "Uh . . . Coach Hathaway?" she asked, doing a slow about-face. "Can I use your phone to call my mom?"

"Sure," Coach Hathaway said. "I'd give you a ride, but the truck's in the shop."

Coach Hathaway went out the back door of the garage and into the yard. When he was gone the three of us just stood around quietly, feeling awkward and dumb—the way people always feel when they've just attacked a baseball special agent in his own garage—then tried to blast him with his own garage-door opener.

Coach Hathaway was gone a while. Knowing him, I bet he had to look for the phone. While I waited I had time to think. I still felt a little wary. Yeah, it seemed like Coach Hathaway was telling the truth, but how could we know for sure? After all it's possible to make an ID card on your computer. On the other hand why would he have done that? He couldn't possibly have expected the three of us to show up in his garage today.

Something else was bugging me, too. I turned to Yasmeen. "Did you really think you were going to level him with that garage-door opener?"

She looked at her shoelaces. "I was scared."

"You looked totally crazy—demented," Sofie said. That made me remember the expression on Yasmeen's face, which made me smile, which made Sofie crack up, which made Yasmeen crack up, too. When Coach Hathaway came back with the phone, he found us all laughing so hard there were tears in our eyes. I think it was the relief we felt that made us get goofy—like we had been scared and upset, and now we weren't anymore, and it felt good.

"It looks as though the mood has lightened somewhat out here," Coach Hathaway said, giving Sofie the phone. "Go ahead and call your mom if you want, Sofie. But if you prefer to wait a few minutes, I've got some milk in the fridge. And there's a fresh box of doughnuts, too."

My stomach growled, and it didn't take

telepathic powers to translate what that meant: Did somebody say doughnuts?

Coach Hathaway's doughnuts had chocolate frosting with red-white-and-blue sprinkles because it was almost Fourth of July. I ate two—one for breakfast and one for lunch—and afterward I felt a lot better.

"Tell me again why I can't have my garage-door opener back." Coach Hathaway was speaking to Yasmeen. He had a dab of white doughnut sugar on his nose, but his face was otherwise clean and his hair was pulled tidily back into its ponytail again.

Yasmeen had already explained once, but she had been kind of vague about just how we came to have the opener—said it came from the park, but nothing more. Now she drained her milk glass before answering, giving Sofie time to cut in: "We took it from the trash bags in the police evidence room."

"*What?*" Coach Hathaway said.

"We only 'borrowed' it—which is why we're taking it back to them. They weren't using it for anything," Sofie said. "We were pretty sure whose-ever garage door it opened—that person had to be the kidnapper."

"Why?" Coach Hathaway asked.

"Because . . ." Sofie started to say, then she stopped. "I have no idea why." She looked at me and Yasmeen. "Why?"

Oh, great. Now what were Yasmeen and I supposed to say? Usually we are careful not to give too much away about our investigation because the information might get back to the criminal himself and help him get away with it. That's how the police work, too. Coach Hathaway must've known what we were thinking.

"Never mind, guys," he said. "I understand. Maybe down the line we'll pool information."

I guess it was the doughnuts making me smarter because sitting at the table I started thinking: A remote control had released the gas and triggered the incendiary device. Coach Hathaway's opener was a remote control. If Coach Hathaway *didn't* put his own opener in the trash at the park, wasn't it an awfully big coincidence for it to be there? Wasn't it too big a coincidence?

So I turned to him and asked, "When did you lose your garage-door opener?"

Coach Hathaway thought for a few seconds. "I usually keep it in the glove compartment of the old junker," he said. "But you know how things are—sometimes I'd take it out, and it'd end up under the seat, or whatever. So I didn't think that much about it when it was gone. I guess I noticed it was missing a couple of months ago, mid-May or so."

"Do you lock your car?" Yasmeen asked.

Coach Hathaway laughed. "No reason to. There's nothing in it but old books."

"So anybody could've gotten in and stolen the opener?" Sofie asked.

"Why would anybody want to steal it?" he asked.

Good question.

When we finished our doughnuts, Sofie called her mom. The plan was for Mrs. Sikora to pick up the three of us, then drop Yasmeen and me at the police station. We had to return the evidence we had "borrowed" before anybody realized it was missing. We said good-bye to Coach Hathaway and thanked him for the doughnuts, then went outside where Mrs. Sikora picked us up.

The ride downtown was quick, not long enough for Mrs. Sikora's nonstop talking to get on my nerves. When she dropped us off at the police station, she mouthed a big *thank you* at me in the rearview mirror. I smiled back at her, but I felt embarrassed. It's not like Yasmeen and I had been exactly good friends to Sofie that day.

"Thanks for the ride!" Yasmeen and I said as the car door slid shut.

It was still hot out, and Yasmeen was in a bad mood. "We better not get caught returning this to the evidence box," she griped. "I never wanted to take the opener in the first place, remember."

"But we learned something when we went to Coach Hathaway's," I said.

Yasmeen refused to be cheered up. "The door opener in the trash . . . Agent K . . . I'm still not totally convinced Coach Hathaway is innocent, either. But if he didn't do it, who did?"

"The person who stole his garage-door opener?" I asked.

"But Coach Hathaway's right. Why would anyone steal it?" Yasmeen asked.

I spoke my thoughts. "Because if you want to kidnap somebody, you can use a door opener as a remote control to release sleeping gas and set off a fire."

"But why not use your *own* opener?" Yasmeen asked. "Why would you take the trouble to steal somebody else's—Coach Hathaway's? *Oh!*"

The thought hit Yasmeen at the same time it hit me. I know because her face got this *omigosh* expression, and for a minute we both stood there so still it was like the sun had frozen us on the sidewalk: *You'd use Coach Hathaway's opener—then leave it at the scene of the crime—because you wanted it to look like Coach Hathaway was the kidnapper!*

And if that was true, we had totally fallen for it. We had played right into the kidnapper's hands.

Chapter Twenty-five

It had been a roller coaster of a day, but Yasmeen and I managed to get lucky about one thing: We returned the opener to the evidence room without anybody figuring out we had borrowed it. Someday, I told myself, I would confess all of this to my mom— someday, that is, when I no longer cared about being permanently grounded from playing video games and watching TV and riding my bike and everything else that makes a kid's life worth living.

Yasmeen and I had a lot to talk over. So we made a plan to meet at Bub's after dinner. Bub is a big fan of old black-and-white mystery movies, and his knowledge of all those old plots helps a lot when we have to sort out evidence.

"Besides," Yasmeen said, "he wants to borrow

some book from my mom. I told him I'd bring it over."

But first there was All-Star practice.

I had barely gotten out of the car at Saucersburg Park when Josh knocked my ball cap off my head so he could get a look at the "big hair" of the kid sleuth who had his picture on the newspaper's front page. I tried to explain about Luau sleeping on my pillow and Yasmeen's mom's mousse, but that just made things worse; and two seconds later the whole team was giving me grief.

Except for Josh and Ari, I didn't even know these guys that well. It was awful.

Then Coach Banner came over. "Break it up, break it up, boys! We've got work to do. You're a team, remember?"

"Aw, let us alone, Dad," Josh said. "We're just havin' fun."

"This is not the time for fun," Coach Banner said. "It's time for—"

"According to you, there's never a time for fun," Josh interrupted him. "You don't even—"

"Josh?" Coach Hathaway tried to smooth things over. "Why don't you and Sergio go on to the—?"

"Hey!" Coach Banner turned on him. "This is between my son and me, okay?"

Now everybody was embarrassed, and we guys started trotting off over to the dugout. It was a crummy start to practice, but then something good happened. Coach Banner was pitching to us for batting practice, and I, Alex Parakeet, slammed one over the right-field fence! I am pretty small for my age and not exactly a power hitter. I had never hit a home run before—not even in practice. Denton, who was catching, jumped up and slapped me on the back; and Coach Banner came trotting in from the mound for a high five.

"Thanks," I said, trying to act modest.

After the ball cleared the fence, it rolled into the far parking lot where an Uncle Sam Lawn Care truck was sitting. Josh was out in the field, and he turned to go get the ball; but he had only gone a couple of steps when Mrs. Banner got out of the truck and picked it up.

"Here, Mom!" Josh hollered. Mrs. Banner took a step, then hauled off and threw the ball smack into the pocket of Josh's glove.

Wow! For a mom she had a pretty good arm.

Dinner was chicken soft tacos with homemade mango salsa. We all sat down, and Mom served herself. "So there was nothing good in all those slimy trash bags?" she asked.

"There was a lot of trash," I said truthfully. "And we did separate out some stuff for Sergeant Ahn. When we talked to him this afternoon, he said he hadn't had a chance to look it over yet." That had been lucky for us. If he had looked at the evidence before we got back, it would have been a problem to sneak the opener back in.

"No surprise there," Mom said. "He's been overwhelmed—we all have. I'll be glad when summer's over, and everyone comes back from vacation."

"How can you say that, Mom?" I asked. "When summer's over, school will start!"

"And baseball will be over, too," Dad said. "That's great you hit one over the fence, Alex!" I had told him about it in the car on the way home.

"Now let's see you do it in a game," my mom said.

"That won't be so easy," I said. "The All-Star pitchers are good, and the best I did in the regular season was a double."

"What is it they say?" Dad asked. "See the ball, hit the ball?"

My dad is a computer dad, not a sports dad. "Did you *ever* play baseball?" I asked him.

"Sure! At recess. Oh—and once in a while in college." Dad looked a little embarrassed all of a sudden.

"In college?" Mom asked. Dad took a couple of bites. Mom looked at him. Then she repeated, "In college?"

"Oh, it's nothing. Just Maggie and I used to play catch now and then, you know, hit the ball in the park and stuff."

"Hmmph," Mom said. "How cute."

"Maggie, Mrs. Banner?" I asked. "That Maggie? She has a great arm!" I explained how she had thrown my home-run ball back to Josh.

"Oh, she was quite the jock in those days," Dad said. "Pitched for the women's softball team. If she'd been a guy, she could've had a pro career— that's what she claimed, at least."

"A jock and brilliant, too!" Mom said. "How did you let her get away, Dan?"

Dad reached across the table and took Mom's hand. "I got a better offer."

When Yasmeen got to my house, Dad suggested we put Luau on his leash and walk him down to Bub's with us.

"Can't he just walk on his own, Dad? He'll follow. He comes with us all the time."

"But I'm afraid he'll stop for snacks," Dad said. "You know, like katydids and june bugs, maybe a cricket or two."

"We'll watch him to be sure he doesn't," I said.

Outside, Yasmeen said, "Your dad's gotten a little crazy with this kitty-on-a-diet deal."

"Tell me about it," I said.

"And he's not the only one," Yasmeen said. "Look at the book Bub wanted." She had been carrying it under her arm, and now she held it out for me to see: *French Women Don't Get Fat.*

"Bub wants a book about French women?" I said.

Yasmeen shrugged. "It has a recipe for leek soup. Leeks are onions, only skinnier. I guess they make a person skinnier, too."

I shook my head. "Everybody *is* going crazy," I said. "What next?"

What next turned out to be the wrong question. I should've said *who's* next. Because the next person to go crazy over diets was none other than my best friend who happens to be a girl, Yasmeen Popp. She was about to turn into a drill sergeant.

Chapter Twenty-six

Even though it was after seven PM, it was light as day out and sticky. I could feel the coating of sweat on my face by the time we got halfway down the block. Pennsylvania weather makes it tough to play baseball sometimes, but I still love summer.

When we got to Bub's, he hollered, "Come on in, it's open," before we even knocked. Luau slipped in behind us and took his regular place on the recliner in front of the TV. Come to think of it, I have never seen anyone other than Luau sitting there. There might as well be a RESERVED FOR KITTY sign on it.

Bub thanked Yasmeen for the book and didn't even look embarrassed when she handed it over. Yasmeen asked how the diet was going.

"Take a look!" Bub said. He stood up from his usual place in the chair at the head of the dining table and turned so we could admire his belly in profile. It could be that Bub's belly was a tiny bit less big and round than before, but it was still plenty big and round.

He was expecting a compliment, but instead Yasmeen said, "Maybe you should get some exercise. I know. We can all go for a walk."

"Exercise is a fine idea, Yasmeen," Bub nodded. "I'll get right on that—tomorrow."

"Not tomorrow. *Now*," Yasmeen said. "We'll all go. We can walk and talk."

"But I got my slippers on already!" Bub argued.

"Don't make excuses!" Yasmeen said, and she took his hand.

Bub laughed. "Okay, okay. You don't have to dislocate my elbow. I'll go quietly. Sheesh." Bub got up from the table and went into his bedroom. A few seconds later he came back. "We can't go after all," he said. "I can't find my good sneakers."

"There's a pair by the front door," Yasmeen said helpfully. "I noticed them when we came in."

"Those are my *old* sneakers," Bub said. "They're wore out."

Sometimes Yasmeen reminds me of my mom,

and this was one of those times. Her arms were folded across her chest, and she had a steely look in her eyes.

Bub sighed. "I guess they're not that old."

Without another word he replaced his slippers with the sneakers. Then he said, "Gimme a second here," and disappeared into the kitchen. Cupboard doors opened and closed, then he came back, and we left out the front door. Luau remained dozing in his recliner.

At the bottom of the steps, Bub whined, "It's too hot for exercise"; but Yasmeen didn't answer, just kept walking. At the end of the driveway, we turned left toward Groundhog Drive, and Yasmeen announced our route: past the elementary school, around Mailbox Park, and home.

"That far?" Bub asked.

"We've got a lot to talk about," Yasmeen said.

She was right. It took a couple of blocks just to bring Bub up to speed. We didn't tell Bub that Coach Hathaway was a special agent for Youth Baseball, only that he was "no longer under suspicion," which is how my mom would say it.

"Well, o' course not," Bub said. His forehead was sweating. "I've known Hank Hathaway for twenty-five years, and he's a good guy—even if his politics are out in left field. So you think somebody mighta stolen his opener?"

"He doesn't lock his car," Yasmeen said. "Because the only thing in it is books."

"It's a sad thought that nobody steals books," Bub said, "but probably true."

"Actually it was the books in his car that made Yasmeen suspect him in the first place." I explained how I saw *The Monkey Wrench Gang* and that it was about ecoterrorism.

"Y'know," Bub said. We were climbing the hill that goes to the park, and he had to speak slowly because he was breathing hard. "Somethin' occurs to me right there." He didn't say anything else, and it was a few seconds before I realized that was because he wasn't there anymore—he had stopped to rest. Yasmeen and I turned back.

"Are you okay?" Yasmeen asked.

"Gotta muster my strength," he said, retrieving something from his pocket.

Yasmeen frowned. "What do you have there?"

"Provisions." Bub displayed a Ziploc bag holding something that looked like trail mix. "You never know when you might get lost and the mounties have to come find you. You don't want to be living off leaves and bark. Want some?"

"There's chocolate chips and M&M'S in there!" Yasmeen said.

"Well, sure!" Bub said. "You gonna eat all that healthy stuff, you gotta have incentive!"

Yasmeen shook her head. "You are never going to lose weight this way. Give it over!" She held out her hand.

I thought Bub would argue, but instead he said, "Okay." Then I saw why. In two big handfuls, he had pretty much emptied the bag. All that was left were two little raisins and some oats in the bottom.

Yasmeen looked at the deflated bag, disgusted. "Come on," she said, nudging Bub's shoulder.

"Okay." Bub was still chewing as we started to walk. "Now that I'm fortified, I can think." He looked down at me, walking beside him. "*You* saw that book in Hank Hathaway's truck, Alex. Likely that somebody else did, too—whoever it was that stole his opener."

"Well, yeah, probably," I said.

Bub nodded. "All right then. The fact he'd be the owner of a book like that gave Yasmeen here a particular idea, the idea ol' Hank might be an ecoterrorist himself. What if it gave our friend the thief that *same* idea? And what if the thief took that idea and ran with it—based a ransom letter on it maybe?"

We got to the top of the hill without even noticing and started down the other side. We were all thinking, trying to put this together.

"You mean," Yasmeen said finally, "that the kidnapper isn't an ecoterrorist at all. That was just a red herring—like the opener in the trash at the park."

"If I'm right," Bub said, "the whole ransom note was a red herring, intended to add to the suspicion that Hank Hathaway was your culprit."

I thought of something else. "It makes a weird kind of sense," I said. "Like if the kidnapper had *really* wanted to get rid of that opener, he could've thrown it a lot farther away than the trash at Saucersburg Park."

"And since it was in the trash at the park, he probably expected the police to find it a lot sooner than now, too," Yasmeen said. "He probably expected Coach Hathaway to be in jail by now!"

"What a nasty thing to do to somebody. What's it called again, Bub?" I asked. "When you try to make it look like somebody else committed a crime?"

"It's whatchacall framing a person," Bub said.

"And it is a nasty thing to do. Is there somebody you kids know who has it in for Coach Hathaway?"

We were in the park now, walking along a dirt trail. The trees were thick on either side, and there were clumps of poison ivy on the ground. The shade would have been nice earlier in the day, but it felt a little dark and scary now as the sun sank.

I could only think of one person who had it in for Coach Hathaway. And I knew Yasmeen must be thinking the same thing. Coach Banner couldn't have kidnapped himself, could he?

Chapter Twenty-seven

When we got back to Bub's house, he collapsed into his usual chair at the head of his table with an *ooof*. I brought him a glass of ice water. He thanked me and looked around. "What happened to your feline, Alex?"

The recliner was empty, so I got up to investigate. I had already been in the kitchen, so I checked the bedrooms and the bathroom. No cat.

Finally I called, "Olly olly oxen free!" and heard an answering *mrrrow*, which meant, *Never play hide-and-seek with a feline, Alex. Felines invented hide-and-seek.*

I followed the sound to the hall closet, opened the door, and there was Luau, resting on a pair of Bub's shoes and batting the laces like they were worms. "Here he is, and he found your good sneakers," I said. Then I scooped him up and brought him back to the table.

"What was he doing in there?" Yasmeen asked.

"Looking for sneakers, I think."

"Is he trying to tell us something?" she asked.

"He was playing with the laces," I said. "Are shoelaces significant?"

"Or is it just that my sneakers smell so good?" Bub asked.

Luau did a quick face wipe, which meant, *Not so much.*

Bub rested his elbows on the table. "So what's your next move, kid sleuths?"

"Coach Banner," Yasmeen said.

"You don't really think—" I said.

"—That he kidnapped himself?" Yasmeen shrugged. "I don't know what to think anymore. Nothing makes sense."

When Bub is thinking hard, he twiddles his thumbs. Now he leaned back in his chair, and the thumbs started some serious spinning. "Is there any way you can take a look around the Banners' house? See if any clues are lying around? I'm wondering if that Red-White-and-Blue formula really does hurt clams."

"It'll be easy to take a look around the Banner house," I said. "There's the team cookout there tomorrow."

"Perfect!" Yasmeen said. "What time?"

Oops. Now what was I supposed to do? I didn't mean to invite Yasmeen to the cookout. It wasn't that I minded having her around, it's just that there was already plenty for the guys to tease me about—I was the worst player on the team, and there was that picture in the paper, too. I didn't need to add the whole girlfriend thing.

I didn't know what to say, so I waited too long to answer. Yasmeen said, "You don't want me to go."

Now I felt bad. "No, it's okay!" I said. "Of course I want you to. The invitation said friends and family."

"But it's your team, all those guys. . . . They'll give you grief about bringing a girl."

They will show no mercy, I thought. But Yasmeen was my best friend who happened to be a girl, and the person I solve mysteries with. "That doesn't matter," I said. I told her the cookout was at four, and we could drive her. "I wish we had a better idea what we're looking for, though," I said.

"Most times, crimes are committed for money,"

Bub said. "Did anyone get any money from Coach Banner's kidnapping?"

"Nobody got anything from Coach Banner being kidnapped—unless . . ." A weird thought crossed my mind—so weird it made me smile.

"What?" Yasmeen asked.

"Well," I said, "we did win that baseball game. So I guess the baseball team got something. Not money but something."

"You think somebody kidnapped Coach Banner so Lawn Care would finally win a game?" Yasmeen asked.

"Too crazy," I said. "But when Bub said 'money,' I remembered all that stuff about paying kids to play baseball. I told you; it was in the newspaper. And I saw that scout in the stands, too."

Bub nodded. "I read that story. Bad idea. I agreed with that coach they quoted—whoever it was. He said pro sports are already about greed and egos. It'd be a shame if that's what sports meant to kids, too."

"I *was* hoping for a fat contract and my own limo," I admitted.

But Bub wasn't listening. He was twiddling his thumbs again. "What scout in the stands?" he asked.

I explained about the guy in the Easter-egg colors, how I thought he must be the one from Nevada that the story mentioned. "Don't guys from Nevada dress flashy like that?" I asked.

"I don't believe I know any guys from Nevada," Bub said. "But I do see at least some slim potential for a money motive there. What if somebody wanted Coach Banner out of the way so that Josh could play that day? So a pro scout could see him and sign him to a big contract like the one Alex is after?"

"That was the day Josh pitched a shutout and hit the big home run, remember?" I said.

Yasmeen nodded. "Memorial Day. It was eventful all around."

"That woulda been a good day for the scout to see him, then," Bub said. "Has he actually been signed to a pro contract, or approached? Have any o' the kids?"

I shook my head. "I don't think so. And I'd probably know because I'm playing with the best local kids, the ones that made the All-Star team."

Bub's thumbs had stopped whirling. He shook his head. "Still though—that money motive. Don't count it out."

"I don't know, Bub," I said after a minute. "If money was the motive—or a pro baseball contract—wouldn't that mean Josh Banner kidnapped his own father?"

As soon as I said it, I wished I hadn't. Both Yasmeen and Bub looked at me like this was a real possibility. Well, was it? Could a kid really do such a thing?

Finally Yasmeen shook her head. "I don't think so," she said. "I mean, is Josh some kind of an explosives genius who knows all about plotting a crime and remote-control devices?"

"Nah," I said, relieved. "He's totally normal except that he's a good athlete. Plus, even if he and his dad don't get along, I don't think he'd actually want to go and kidnap him and lock him up in a Porta Potty for a day. I mean, I get mad at my dad, too, but I wouldn't go that far."

Chapter Twenty-eight

To get to the Banners' house, you drive out past Saucersburg, turn off the highway on a narrow road for a while, then drive up a long driveway past a tennis court—the Banners' very own tennis court.

"Talk about ostentatious," Mom said from the front seat.

"Yeah!" I said as we drove past the huge front yard, which was as tidy and bright as a putting green. "Isn't it great?"

Dad was driving. I was sitting in the backseat behind Mom. She looked around and narrowed her eyes at me.

"What?" I asked.

Yasmeen, sitting next to me, laughed. "Ostentatious is *not* a virtue, bud."

"Why not?" I asked. The house came into view after we went over a little hill. It was massive, too, and white—three stories high. It reminded me of a bakery cake.

Dad steered the car around a fountain in the middle of a circular driveway that went to the front door. "I remember there was some nickname for the house at the time it was being built," he said. "The house that . . . what was it? Hypno-something? Oh, I know—hypnoheptadine. 'The House that Hypnoheptadine Built.'"

"What's hypno . . . what-you-said?" I asked.

It was Mom who answered. "It's the proper name for that formula Mrs. Banner invented— Red-White-and-Blue formula."

Dad pulled the car in behind some others I recognized from baseball. "How do you know all that?" he asked her.

Mom ignored him and looked back at me. "Coach Banner hasn't said anything to you about the case, has he, Alex? At practice?"

"Uh-uh." I shook my head.

"That's good." Mom nodded. "I have kept them up-to-date when there was anything to report. But as far as they can tell, I guess we haven't made much progress."

Dad turned off the motor. "'As far as they can tell'?" he asked.

Mom didn't answer this time, either, and we all climbed out of the car and started walking toward the house. There were white pillars on either side of the front doors, which were inset with fancy colored glass.

"Noreen?" Dad said when we got to the door. "Is there something they don't know?"

Mom had a strange expression on her face, like she was trying not to have any expression at all. Finally she said, "Let's just enjoy the cookout, shall we?"

Yasmeen and I looked at each other. Something was up with Mom.

Dad rang the bell, and a few moments later Coach Banner let us in with a big, friendly welcome.

"Feel free to have a look around," he said. "Some of the guys are in back playing croquet, and there's another pack of 'em on the deck with the food. The adults seem to have congregated in the family room. I'm on my way out to the barbecue."

My parents headed for the family room, while Yasmeen and I decided to take Coach Banner up on his offer and do a quick walk-through. Maybe some clues were lying around waiting for us. The front hallway kind of reminded me of the entrance to a museum—only there was no information desk. Overhead was a chandelier with a ton of dangling little prism-deals. In the rest of the house, everything seemed shiny, too—the doorknobs, the wood floors, the counters. There were so many flat-screen TVs, I couldn't count them all. The mud room, which was at the far end of the kitchen, was bigger than my bedroom, and in it were about a thousand pairs of shoes—sneakers, rain boots, hiking boots, clogs. I even recognized one pair—the red-white-and-blue bicycle shoes Uncle Sam always wears to ride his bike at the Memorial Day run. With their glittery red laces, they were pretty spiffy looking.

But if any clues were waiting around for Yasmeen and me, we were too dazzled to notice. Finally we went outside on the deck where Sam, Sergio, Ari, and Denton from my team were dedicating some quality time to some quality junk food. It took about five seconds till somebody—Sam—asked if Yasmeen was my girlfriend, and then Denton remembered we had been on the cover of the magazine and in the newspaper together—so that kicked off more razzing about kid sleuths and celebrity couples.

Luckily Ari knows Yasmeen from our neighborhood, and he's used to us being friends. He acted normal about her being there, and that made the teasing die down.

We talked about baseball, and I ate some cookies, and some popcorn, and some chips, and a couple of grapes for health. Then Ari said he hoped Coach Banner would let Josh play more than he did in the regular season.

"Where is Josh, anyway?" Sergio asked.

"Down there," Denton pointed. "See him? Playing croquet across the lawn."

"You want to go down there and play?" Ari asked Yasmeen. "Croquet's a girl game, isn't it?"

Yasmeen gave him a look.

Ari looked at his shoelaces. "I was only asking."

"I'll play," Sergio said, "even if it is a girl game."

The four guys grabbed last handfuls of chips, then took off in a herd, stomping down the stairs from the deck to the patio, then the backyard.

"We can go, too, if you want," Yasmeen said. "I like croquet."

"We are supposed to be investigating," I said, "And I don't think the clues are way out there."

Yasmeen grinned. "Okay, come on. Let's go listen in on the grown-ups."

There were a few parents outside where the barbecue grill was, but most of them were standing around in the family room by the kitchen, talking and drinking wine or beer. My mom was talking to Mrs. Banner and drinking coffee. She doesn't like to drink anything else when she might get called to go to work, which is pretty much all the time.

The parent food was mostly cheese, fruit, and healthy-looking bread with seeds. Yasmeen and I got some watermelon on a plate and took a seat on a sofa facing a TV set that was turned off, away from the food table. It had a high back so we could eavesdrop, and nobody could see us.

". . . extensively tested," Mrs. Banner was saying to my mom. I could tell from her voice she was chewing. "I should know, I formulated it myself," she added.

"Really, Maggie?" my mom said. "I didn't know that."

I looked at Yasmeen and shrugged—*what gives?* They had to be talking about Red-White-and-Blue formula, didn't they? And my mom did *too* know Mrs. Banner invented it.

"Oh, yes," Mrs. Banner said. "I had an inkling about some of the research I was doing, how it might be useful in a practical application. So I quit my job at the college to pursue it, and . . . well, I guess I got lucky."

"How *does* it work, exactly?" my mom asked. "Red-White-and-Blue formula, I mean?"

"It promotes the growth of healthy grass," Mrs. Banner said, "by retarding the growth of the competing fauna."

"Ahhh," my mom said thoughtfully. "You mean it kills bugs. So would it kill clams, too? Clams in the Chesapeake Bay?"

Sometimes my mom seems like she has different identities for different situations. Like there's the mom identity, the wife identity, the cop identity. . . . Right now she wasn't the party mom at all. She sounded more like the cop.

And Mrs. Banner sounded annoyed. "Please, Noreen. You don't believe the kidnapper who sent that preposterous letter? Honestly, sometimes those ecology nuts just make me sick."

Mom backed off. "It's not that I believe the letter. But I have heard about lawn chemicals that pollute water, and I have heard of other instances of problems, too."

"What have you heard?" Mrs. Banner asked.

"Perhaps this isn't the time . . ." Mom said.

I thought: Yes, it is, too, the time, Mom! Keep asking questions!

Mrs. Banner sighed. "No, no—go ahead," she said. "It's my business you're talking about here, and next to Josh my business is my baby. I'm proud of it."

"I understand," Mom said. "I feel that way about my job, too. Proud. Anyway, it's only that my neighbor . . . Well, she mentioned to me her dog had to go to the vet—I guess he got quite sick—and she blamed an application of your lawn formula."

"I think I know the woman you mean. The one who never shuts up?"

Suddenly I knew who they were talking about, too. Mrs. Sikora! She had said something about their dog that day when she gave us the ride. They couldn't wake him up.

"She's called us, too," Mrs. Banner was saying, "and she's quite mistaken. The active ingredient in Red-White-and-Blue is very safe."

"Hypnoheptadine, isn't it?" Mom asked.

There was a pause—long enough that I considered peeking over the back of the sofa to see what was going on. But before I had a chance, Mrs. Banner said, "Why, yes. But, Noreen, didn't you say just now that you didn't know anything about Red-White-and-Blue formula?"

Mom ignored her question. "I went through a bad patch with insomnia a couple of years ago, and I tried Beddy-Bye. I'm a big label reader, so I noticed the active ingredient in that is hypnoheptadine, too. I guess with your Red-White-and-Blue, the bugs just get sleepy and never know what hit them." Mom laughed, and Mrs. Banner joined her, but Mrs. Banner's laugh was kind of shrill.

I don't know about Yasmeen, but I was thinking Mom was about one question away from accusing Mrs. Banner of kidnapping her own husband. Who would know better how to knock out a husband than the wife who invented the formula? But there was still the little question of why Mrs. Banner would want to kidnap Mr. Banner and knock him out. Was Bub right? Did it have something to do with money? Well, whatever it was, we could sort out the details later. I had one other question for right now: Is it polite for a party guest to slap handcuffs on her hostess?

But Mom's interrogation never got that far. A second later I heard another voice—somebody else's mom—butting in. "Can you believe the All-Star uniforms are going to have *white* pants?"

"Oh, I *know*!" Mrs. Banner said, and you have never heard anybody more eager to talk about white baseball pants. "How are we supposed to keep them clean?"

"Especially if the team keeps winning, and we have to travel," the other mom said. "Do we take detergent to the hotels, or what?"

I looked at Yasmeen. Her teeth were clenched shut. She was just as frustrated by this change of conversation topic as I was. What followed was some unbelievably boring talk about the stain-fighting qualities of sprays, soaks, and sticks. Finally the other mom laughed and said, "I'm just grateful we don't have to wash their shoes!"

I can't be sure, but I think I actually heard Yasmeen's mouth drop open. Then after the tiniest pause, she was on her feet, yanking my arm and saying: *"Come on, Alex! Hurry!"*

At the Banners' huge house, the sprint from the family room to the mud room is about one mile. My dad claims I am just as smart as Yasmeen, but that day it didn't seem like it. Just as my legs strained to keep up, so did my brain.

"The lab . . ." Yasmeen kept looking back at me and trying to explain. "The hypnoheptadine . . . the residue? It's on Uncle Sam's bike shoes! Hurry, Alex!"

With pathetic slowness I put it together: The

gas that put Coach Banner to sleep in the Porta Potty would have left some trace on his shoes. And the shoes—we had just seen them in the mud room!

I was out of breath by the time we got to the kitchen, which is gleaming white and silver like a mad scientist's laboratory.

"You grab them," I said to Yasmeen as we ran by the refrigerator. "You're faster in case you have to make a getaway."

"No getaway," Yasmeen said as we passed the oven. "We *casually* steal the shoes. We *casually* walk out of the house—like nothing's unusual."

We rounded the breakfast nook, and the door to the mud room was in sight. I passed Yasmeen, spun around, and pushed through the swinging door backward. "Watch out in case—" I started to say, but the look on Yasmeen's face shut me up.

I turned around.

"Hello, Yasmeen. Hello, Alex." Mrs. Banner was standing in the middle of the room—between us and the back door. She was holding the spangled bike shoes by their red laces, like a hunting trophy. "Looking for something?" she asked.

Chapter Twenty-nine

Mrs. Banner had kidnapped her own husband.

Yasmeen and I knew it.

Mrs. Banner knew we knew it.

For a few seconds we stood in the mud room doorway staring at her like we were paralyzed. Then we mumbled something about how we were sorry, we musta gotten lost, see ya later, bye, and we backed out of there like scared rabbits.

After that we spent a miserable hour trying to pretend we were normal kids at a normal cookout while at the same time we did our total best to avoid running into Mrs. Banner. The only good thing—if you could call it that—was that Mrs. Banner knew as well as we did the bike shoes were our last hope of proving she did it. Since she had the shoes, we weren't much of a threat. That meant she'd leave us alone.

Didn't it?

A few minutes before it was time to go home, Yasmeen whispered, "Are we going to tell your mom?"

I had been worrying about the same thing. "Not right now," I whispered back. "I'm still hoping we can avoid telling her about how we borrowed the clicker."

"She's almost got the case figured out anyway," Yasmeen said. "Maybe she'll think of another angle—something we've forgotten."

"I sure hope so," I said.

In bed before I went to sleep, I explained everything to Luau—how we overheard the conversation between Mom and Mrs. Banner, how we confronted Mrs. Banner in the mud room. Sometimes with a cat it's hard to tell if he's listening or snoozing, but for once, as Luau lay on my chest, I could see he was paying attention. He even kept his eyes open.

"Mrs. Banner must have set it all up the night before—rigged the gas in the Porta Potty and fixed the other ones so they looked occupied when they weren't. Then, on Memorial Day she used the Uncle Sam's Lawn Care truck to move the Porta Potty with Coach Banner in it over to the other side of the park," I told Luau. "That was while everyone was watching the fireworks or trying to put out the fire. After that she went home, switched cars, and came back, acting all upset that her husband was missing. She was even crying!"

Luau mrffed, *What about the garage-door opener?*

"She must have been planning the whole thing for a long time," I said. "She didn't like Henry Hathaway or his politics, so she framed him— made it look like he did it. When she stole the door opener out of his truck, she saw the book and got the idea of putting the ecoterrorist thing into the ransom note, too. Probably she thought mentioning Red-White-and-Blue formula in the note was like a double guarantee that nobody would think to consider her a suspect. With the door opener, she could have dropped it in the trash anytime after she used it to set off the explosion and release the hypno-hupto . . . hypno-hopto . . . hypno-hippo . . . the whatever-it's-called."

I shook my head. "I just wish we had thought of the bike shoes sooner—before she did!"

Luau shifted his weight and swished his tail. *I think, Alex, that you're forgetting something else.*

Have you ever noticed that yawns are catching? I yawned, and a second later Luau did too. "Yeah," I mumbled, "probably. But what is it?"

Luau didn't answer. I think he was asleep.

My mom had to work the Fourth of July holiday. I really hoped she was working on the kidnapping.

Yasmeen spent the Fourth of July day doing family stuff, but I knew she and her parents and Jeremiah were planning to come to the game and the fireworks at Saucersburg Park afterward. A lot of other people from my neighborhood were coming, too. The fireworks are a tradition.

At my house Dad made pancakes for breakfast; then the two of us went on a long bike ride out to a swimming hole we know. Dad called it "father-son bonding time," which must be something that comes out of those how-to-raise-a-perfect-kid books he's always reading.

By the time Dad and I got home, I had to hurry to get ready to go to the park for warm-ups. I changed into my uniform, then grabbed my base-ball bag. As I picked the bag up, a cloud of orange cat fur rose around me. Luau was nowhere to be seen, but earlier he must have decided my baseball bag was a cozy place for a nap. I looked inside to make sure my cleats and everything were in place—they were. Then I hurried down to the garage so Dad could drive me.

The first five-and-a-half innings of the Fourth of July game against Marion Run didn't go so well for the College Springs All-Stars. When the field lights were turned on at eight-thirty, we were heading into the home half of the sixth behind, 3–1. We would get one more chance; but unfortunately the bottom of the batting order, including yours truly, was coming up.

Of course all we needed to win was for Ari and Denton to get on base, and then for me to hit a home run.

As an extra bonus this would make me—for once—the hero.

Yeah, right. And after that fairy tale, we'd all live happily ever after.

Marion Run's closer was a big left-hander who threw kind of erratically but hard. Ari watched the first pitch go by high and outside, ball one. I was in the dugout. I couldn't see that well, so I stood up—and felt my right shoelace break. I dropped back down to the bench to tie it, thinking it was kind of weird it would break. Didn't Dad buy me new ones at the end of the regular season?

I heard the ball hit the catcher's glove again and the umpire call, "*Stee-rike!*" One and one.

I tried to tie the lace to itself to fix it, but the way it had broken, this was not so easy to do. In fact it seemed like my shoelace had been attacked by some wild creature or something. It was practically shredded. Next to me on the bench, Josh looked over.

"Shoelace?" he asked. "My dad keeps spares in his bag. I can go get it from the truck if you want. I'm not doin' anything else—like, you know, batting."

"Oh, yeah. I remember about the laces," I said. "Your dad always has—" I stopped. Shoelaces. Coach Banner and shoelaces . . .

And then it hit me. On Memorial Day, right before he was kidnapped, Coach Banner had sat down with Yasmeen and me and threaded silver shoelaces into his bike shoes. *But the laces on the shoes last night had been red.* Where were the silver ones? Wherever they were, wouldn't they have traces of hypnoheptadine?

Josh asked, "Dude? You okay? You've got a really weird expression on your face."

"Does your dad keep those silver shoelaces in his bag? The laces from Memorial Day?"

Josh just looked at me like I was crazy. "Silver shoelaces from Memorial Day? Shoot, dude, how do I know?"

I jumped off the bench, one shoe untied, and tripped my way to the steps that lead out of the dugout. "I gotta go," I said, calling out to the guys in general as I bumped them out of my way. "I mean—I'll be right back. Uh . . . if I miss my at-bat, tell Coach I broke my leg or something."

And out into the night I went.

Mom had been too late to get the Uncle Sam costume, and Yasmeen and I had been too late to get the shoes. But this time I was not going to be too late. If the silver laces were in that gym bag, I was going to get them—before Mrs. Banner did.

Chapter Thirty

Coach Banner always parks his truck in the dirt lot down the bank behind the field. I was stumbling in the dark to get there when I heard hooting from some of our fans, which probably meant Ari had drawn a walk. Part of my head was still in the game. Now if only Denton could get on . . . But it wouldn't be me with a chance to be the hero. It would probably be . . . I had to think about it. Josh? The subbing rules in PYB are so complicated even the coaches have a hard time keeping them straight, but I was pretty sure Josh would be eligible to bat now that I broke my leg and everything.

I spotted Sam Banner's truck in the second row of the lot. After what happened last night, I half expected to see Mrs. Banner there, holding up the shoelaces in triumph—ha-ha-ha once again.

But she wasn't there. Nobody was. And the parking lot was beyond the spill of the ball-field lights, so it was plenty dark here, too.

I didn't know how to work the latch of the tailgate, so I put my foot on the trailer hitch and pushed my body up and over into the truck bed. I saw Coach Banner's gym bag—the one with the United States Marine Corps insignia on it—right away. I took one last look around, then unzipped the bag and reached inside. If you reached into my gym bag in the dark, you'd come up with a fossilized lunch, sticky crumbs, and ancient dirty socks. In Coach Banner's gym bag, I felt only baseballs, neatly bunched clean socks, a box of power bars, and some plastic bags. In one of those bags were the shoelaces, but which bag? I couldn't see, so I flipped the whole gym bag over and was dumping it out when I heard footsteps on the gravel—footsteps coming toward the truck.

I ducked down, lying with my face on the bed of the truck where the plastic bags had fallen— and now I saw the one with shoelaces in it. Silver shoelaces? It was too dark to tell.

I grabbed the plastic bag and clenched it in

my fist. I wanted to run like heck toward the bleachers and give it to my mom, but something told me to stay where I was. Whoever was walking around in the parking lot was still there. I could hear footsteps and beyond them the sounds of the game—a cheer from the home bleachers, from *our* fans. It wasn't loud enough to be a run, but a base hit? Were both Denton and Ari on base now?

Then a woman's voice very nearby said, "Come on out of there, Alex."

Mrs. Banner.

You know how when you were little you thought you could close your eyes and disappear, and the monsters wouldn't get you? I think for a second that's what I tried to do.

"This minute, young man."

Reluctantly I opened my eyes a squinch. Mrs. Banner was standing behind the truck, looking at me over the tailgate. In the dark her face, framed by her dark hair, looked spooky pale.

I closed my eyes again.

"I was one step ahead of you and your girlfriend last night," she said. "You're one step ahead of me now. But one step won't be enough."

"I won't come out," I said in a squeaky cartoon-character voice that didn't sound like my own. "You'll have to come in and get me."

I didn't say that because I'm brave. I was just stating a fact. If I could stall her a little longer, the game would end, and then people would start moving around—some of them coming out to this parking lot—maybe.

"Alex, I don't want to have to do something we'll both regret," Mrs. Banner said. "Give me the shoelaces, and it will be my word against yours. You won't be able to prove a thing. Otherwise . . ."

Otherwise, what?

Against my better judgment I opened my eyes. Mrs. Banner was holding something up for me to see. It was so dark I could only make out the silhouette against the sky. At first I thought it was a pen, but then I realized it was something mightier—a hypodermic needle.

"Hypnoheptadine," she said as calmly as if she were teaching a class, "is a remarkable narcotic. Any way you take it—drink it, breathe it, or inject it—you go right to sleep. And there's something else, too. It reliably induces amnesia." She smiled. "Alex, you won't remember a thing."

With that, the truck's tailgate dropped, and I felt a firm grip on my ankle.

"No!"

I tried to kick free, but Mrs. Banner's grip was like a manacle; and in spite of all my struggling, she succeeded in pulling me toward her. Inch by inch my rear end was approaching that needle. It seemed hopeless, but then I heard the *crack* of bat against baseball, a gasp from the baseball crowd, a pause, and . . . wild cheering!

Home run!

The College Springs All-Stars win the game!

"That was Josh!" I said. "Had to be!"

"What?" Mrs. Banner turned her head toward the field, and her death grip loosened enough that my ankle broke free. I skittered backward toward the truck cab and huddled there, making myself as tiny as possible. I was cornered, but at least my rear wasn't so accessible anymore.

Mrs. Banner clenched her fist. "That's my boy!" Then she sighed. "I did it all for him."

I wanted to keep her talking. "What do you mean?"

"He had to play so the pro scout would see him. I knew Sam would never let him play, so what else could I do? I had to get rid of Sam. And he came through, didn't he—my Josh? Hit the longest home run anyone around here ever saw."

I knew the answer to this next question, but all I could think about was stalling her. "What pro scout?"

Mrs. Banner didn't mind answering—amnesia would make me forget this conversation anyway—but she didn't want to be stalled. While she spoke she climbed into the truck bed. "The guy with the rainbow fashion sense. He's a scout for the new youth league. Has to be." She crawled toward me. "All the games he goes to? The note-taking? The way he dresses?" I could feel her breath. "My son is going to have the athletic career I never had."

Like a snake striking she reached—and the next second the needle was poised above my precious white uniform pants. "Don't fight, Alex," she said. "It will hurt a lot more if you fight."

I was wondering just how much it would hurt when a familiar, breathy, girl voice asked, "Hey, hi, uh . . . what are you guys doing anyway?"

Then a second voice chimed in: "Did Alex step on a nail? Does he need a tetanus shot?"

"Ashley! Teresa! *Help!*" I shouted.

Mrs. Banner knew when she was licked. She dropped the needle, sprang lightly over the side of the truck, and ran like the athlete she used to be. But there was one thing Mrs. Banner didn't count on: how fast Ashley could move when she wasn't giggling. Ashley sprinted, Ashley dodged, Ashley sidestepped between two cars—then Ashley jumped into Mrs. Banner's path and stuck out her foot.

Mrs. Banner might have avoided it—if she had seen it. But she never did. She was distracted by a shadow that had appeared out of nowhere, a shadow that came toward her head-on, moving fast. Going full throttle Mrs. Banner tumbled over Ashley's foot and careened forward—right into the outstretched arms of the shadow—who by now had materialized into Yasmeen Popp.

"Hold her, Yasmeen!" Ashley yelled.

"Don't let her go!" Teresa added.

"Sit on her!" said a fourth girl-voice, one it took me a second to recognize. Sofie Sikora? How did she get here?

Chapter Thirty-one

From my seat on the tailgate of the pickup, I watched Sofie go for help, then return with my mom, both of them running. Mom relieved Yasmeen, Teresa, and Ashley of Mrs. Banner, then clapped handcuffs on her. Was it weird for my mom to be arresting my dad's ex-girlfriend? She didn't have much time to think about that. Right away All-Stars from both teams started coming down the slope from the ball field and fanning out in the parking lot. Behind them came what seemed like the combined populations of Marion Run, Saucersburg, and greater College Springs, including my dad and Bub and Jeremiah and almost everyone else who lives on my street.

All these people had come here tonight for the

fireworks display, and now as a special bonus they would get to witness a kidnapper being carted off to jail. It was better than TV.

Yasmeen, Sofie, and Dad wanted the whole story, so I gave it to them as best I could. My heart was still pounding, my palms were clammy with sweat, and every time I blinked that syringe full of hypnoheptadine did a dance in front of my eyeballs. Dad gave me a big bear hug, which helped.

"Why did you come down here anyway?" I asked Yasmeen. "And you, Sofie? I mean, Ashley and Teresa were just making their usual tour of the ball field, but you guys . . . ?"

"When you didn't take your at-bat, I knew something was wrong," Yasmeen said. "So I came to look."

Sofie shrugged and said, "Same here. Only," she looked over at Yasmeen, "we weren't fast enough."

"Yeah, you were. You caught her!" I said.

"*They* caught her." Yasmeen nodded at Ashley and Teresa, who for once didn't giggle. "If you'd had to wait for either one of us, you'd be sound asleep right now, and Mrs. Banner'd be halfway home with the shoelaces."

I guessed that was true. My rescuers were

Ashley and Teresa—two girly girls who thought Yasmeen was stuck-up.

"Thanks," I told them.

Now they giggled.

A minute later Mom came over with Mrs. Banner in tow, and I had to fill her in on everything that had happened. Mrs. Banner just stood there like a stone, her face with no expression at all. Mom, meanwhile, put her arm around me like she wouldn't be letting go anytime soon.

We were all waiting for Officer Krichels to show up in the patrol car when Yasmeen said, "Look—it's that guy! The pro baseball scout!"

Sure enough, making his way toward us was the Easter-egg man. Tonight—in honor of the holiday, I guess—his shirt was red, and his jacket was white. He had a tie, too—with stars and stripes.

Who was he, anyway?

Mom looked up. "Hey, Mark."

"Noreen," he said.

"You *know* him?" I asked her.

"Mark Verde," she said. "My son, Alex."

"You're a darned good player, Alex," he said. "I've enjoyed coming to the games."

Visions of the major leagues danced in my

head. "Really? Do you think I've got big-league potential? Are you gonna sign me?"

Mr. Verde looked confused. "Sign you? Sorry?" He looked at my mom.

My mom shrugged. "I'm afraid Mr. Verde isn't in any position to sign you, Alex. He works for the federal government. He and I have been working on a little project together. That's one reason I've been so busy."

"The project with the feds!" I said. "But since when does the government pay baseball players?"

My mom frowned. "What are you talking about, Alex?"

Now Mrs. Banner spoke. "Are you saying you're *not* a baseball scout?"

Even though Mr. Verde liked to wear bright colors, he had the kind of face you could tell didn't smile much, and his voice when he answered was dead serious. "No, ma'am, I'm not a baseball scout. I'm with the EPA—Environmental Protection Agency. I've been in town off and on for some weeks now, collecting data on Red-White-and-Blue formula, your lawn care company, and you yourself, Mrs. Banner. When Detective Parakeet gets done, I'll have a few questions for you, too."

While we had been talking, Coach Banner had

been coming toward us through the crowd. This was lucky because at that moment Mrs. Banner's knees buckled, and in the nick of time, Coach reached out and steadied her.

"But the baseball games?" she asked weakly, leaning on Coach Banner. "What were you doing at all those baseball games?"

Mr. Verde shrugged. "There's no mystery, ma'am. I miss my kid when I'm away like I've been. He's a tremendous little ballplayer—a short-stop. Going to these PYB games has been the next best thing to being home."

"But . . . the clipboard? The notes?"

Mr. Verde looked embarrassed. "What can I say, ma'am? I'm a nerd from way back. Game's a lot more fun for me if I keep a scorecard."

"Me, too!" said Jeremiah. "I calculate Alex at .336 for the season. What've you got?"

Mr. Verde turned to answer, and after that the two of them kept busy comparing stats. I don't think they even noticed when the crowd stirred, and someone shouted, "Make way!"

A police car with its red light flashing was turning into the park. A few seconds later it pulled up beside us and stopped. Officer Krichels came around from the driver's side to open the rear door for Mrs. Banner, and she slumped in. She looked small, sad, and alone in the backseat. What she did was terrible, but it still seemed mean for all these people to be watching at a time like this.

"Noreen—Detective Parakeet?" Coach Banner said. "Can I ride with her? I think she needs . . ." He shrugged.

Mom raised her eyebrows and started to say, "After what she did . . . ?"; but then she thought again, closed her mouth, and sighed. "DA's not gonna like it," she said, "but okay."

"What about Josh?" I asked.

"Hank's got him." Coach Banner looked me in the eye. "Maybe this isn't the time, Alex, but then again there won't be a better one. Hank and I have our differences, but, well . . . Let me show you." He was wearing a warm-up jacket. Which he unzipped and opened out to reveal a badge just like Coach Hathaway's. "Pennsylvania Youth Baseball. Special Agent Q."

I couldn't believe it, and apparently it was news to Mrs. Banner as well. "What's the meaning of this, Sam?" she asked, sounding a little more like her usual self.

"Baseball the way these kids play it is a beautiful thing, Maggie, sport for its own sake," he said.

"But how long will that last if money gets involved? Someone's gotta protect the kids."

When the police car pulled away a few minutes later, Coach Banner was sitting beside his wife in the backseat. It was right about then that I noticed my right arm was aching, and that's when I realized I was still gripping the plastic bag of shoelaces from Coach Banner's gym bag.

I held them out to my mom. "The shoelaces. You need them. They're the clue I risked my life, or at least my, uh . . . derriere for."

Mom examined the bag. "Tough to see out here in so little light, and I can't open the bag till I've got gloves. But best I can tell right now, all these laces are either black or white."

"The silver ones have got to be in there!" I said. "Otherwise, why was Mrs. Banner so determined to take them from me?"

"Mrs. Banner might have made a mistake," Mom said. "After all, she made a mistake about Mark Verde's occupation—a very big mistake."

Chapter Thirty-two

With all that had happened that night, the Saucersburg organizers said there would be a delay before the fireworks could begin.

"Please be patient," said the voice on the crackly PA.

Mom had gone downtown to interrogate Mrs. Banner, but Yasmeen, Dad, and I were sitting together on the top row of the baseball bleachers. Sofie and her little brother, Byron, were in the row below us with Bub, Ashley, and Teresa. Jeremiah was sitting with his parents down in the front row with Sofie's mom and Mr. Stone, who also lives on our street. It seemed like almost everyone had come to Saucersburg Park for the Fourth.

Yasmeen had been real quiet ever since

Mrs. Banner was taken away. I thought I knew why, too, because I felt the same—not happy like I should have been with the mystery solved. I guess I was shocked at what a terrible thing a person, a *mom*, had done because she thought it would help her kid get a big baseball career.

Finally I told Yasmeen what I was thinking. "I don't feel mad at her exactly," I said. "I mean, she was going to stick a needle in me—but in a way she did it because she loves Josh. She wanted him to have a chance to be a great baseball player."

"That's garbage," Yasmeen said—pronouncing it gar-bawzh. "She didn't do it for Josh. She did it because she wanted more money and more success, and she expected him to earn it for her. She's greedy! Look at that house! Nobody needs a house like that!"

"Are you kidding?" I said. "It would be great to have a house like that! All those TVs? Video games in every room!"

This was one argument I thought I could win. But before we really got into it, a voice below and behind me called: "Hey, kids! Congrats and all that! Another victory for truth and justice, thanks to the kid sleuths. Can I get a few words for my readers? And a picture of the two of

245

you? If it's lit by fireworks—man! That'd be a prizewinner!"

Yasmeen grinned and swiveled her head around. "Hi, Mr. Roberts! Be right there!" She grabbed hold of the bar at the top of the bleachers, planning to swing down and talk to *The Middle Daily Times'* ace reporter, but then—like she'd just thought of something—she dropped her hands again.

"Uh . . . Alex?" she said slowly. "Do you think I'm stuck-up?"

I looked at her. Was she thinking about that day in the caf? I never thought what the other girls said had bothered her. "Of course not," I said loyally.

She smiled. "Thanks, bud. But . . . well, what do you think if this time we don't hog all the glory?"

When, I wondered, was it me who wanted to hog glory in the first place? But I said, "I've totally had my picture in the paper enough."

Yasmeen nodded. "Me, too. Hey, Mr. Roberts!" she called down. "I've got a better idea." Then she leaned over and tapped Sofie Sikora's shoulder. "Get Ashley and Teresa," she told Sofie. "There's a guy here who wants to talk to you."

* * *

Tim Roberts must have had a whole lot of questions—or maybe the girls had a whole lot of answers—because they were still talking half an hour later when Mom surprised all of us and showed up back at the park. By now there had been an announcement that the show would start soon, and we were all expecting the first *kaboom* anytime.

"I couldn't miss the fireworks!" Mom said, as she settled in next to me. If this was supposed to explain her being there—well, it didn't. My mom is always missing out on stuff because of work.

"Why are you here really?" I asked.

Mom looked at me and Dad on one side of her, then at Yasmeen on the other. When she spoke she kept her voice low so the whole town wouldn't hear. "Maggie Banner's talking to her lawyer now, but she's already made a statement. I've got to give her credit," Mom said. "It was an ingenious plan. There was an old garage door opener at the lawn care warehouse, and she set the dip-switches on its receiver to align with Coach Hathaway's remote. Then she rigged that receiver to a gas canister in the Porta Potty. When she pressed the button on the remote it tripped the relay that would normally power the door opener's motor but in this case it opened a solenoid valve."

I looked at my dad. "Do you understand that?"

"Never let it be said that I am dumber than your dad's ex-girlfriend."

"Of course not," Dad said.

"I feel so bad for Josh," I said.

"What'll happen to her?" Yasmeen asked.

"I don't know for sure," Mom said. "But sometimes a crisis is a blessing in disguise. Sam doesn't want to break up his family, and if he can forgive her, I think the judge will be lenient. A lot of times people are sentenced to community service—cleaning up litter, for example."

"What about the EPA investigation?" Dad asked.

"Ironic, isn't it?" Mom said. "When Maggie Banner wrote the fake ransom letter, she had no idea her lawn care formula really was being investigated by the EPA. From what she said, she really believes it's harmless. If it turns out it does kill clams, the feds will probably levy a big fine against Uncle Sam's Lawn Care. My bet is the Banners won't always have such a big house."

I had one final question. "What about the shoelaces, Mom? Were they even in that bag?"

Mom smiled. "You risked your tush for nothing, kid. Coach Banner keeps the Uncle Sam shoelaces in a box at home. Luckily, Maggie didn't know that any more than you did. When the fireworks are over, I'll run out to their house and get them. Then I'll head downtown to log them into evidence."

"Wait a minute, Noreen," Dad said. "How come *you* have to do all that? Can't Fred do something for once? It's a holiday, for gosh sake, and you work all the time!"

"I know." Mom looked kind of embarrassed. "But I told Fred he could knock off for the night. He has to get up really early tomorrow, you know. He and Bub have a jogging date. There's a race scheduled for Labor Day, and the two of them . . ."

The rest of Mom's sentence was drowned out by the *boom, pop, sizzle* of the first bouquet of fireworks. We all looked up at once, so our faces glowed in the golden light. There was something pretty great about all of us together on the Fourth of July this way—girly girls and smart girls, guys with shiny SUVs and guys with rusty pickup trucks, professors who have read every book and coal miners who have seen every movie—a bunch of people who disagree about war and peace and politics but know they have to get along because they depend on one another—kind of like a baseball team. I had the goofy thought that maybe that was what patriotism was about. One of these days—when things get back to normal—I'll ask Uncle Sam.

It was midnight when I pushed Luau off my pillow and collapsed into bed. "You missed the excitement!" I said.

Luau rolled onto his back, exposing his orange tummy, which was as round as ever. When I scratched it, he mrrfed, *Excitement is overrated.*

"No, really," I told him. "I was almost injected, then we won the game and the girls rescued me and Mrs. Banner went to jail and Mr. Verde turned out to be—" I yawned. "Which reminds me—Luau, was it you that destroyed the shoelaces on my cleats? Because when my shoelace broke is when—"

Luau interrupted. *Alex, this is all very interesting, but can it wait? A cat as good-looking as I am needs a lot of beauty sleep.*

I closed my eyes. "Okay, fine," I mumbled. "But in the morning, you've got some explaining to do."